Praise for *Touching the Shadows*

Most of us don't know it when we sign up for marriage, but it is *holy* love that God intends for us in its blessing. Bruce Nygren's bold, articulate, honest narration of his marriage as it is saved by suffering documents in detail just such a Christ-formed holy love.

—EUGENE H. PETERSON
Author and translator of *The Message*

Touching the Shadows is a moving celebration of commitment in marriage—no matter what the circumstances or cost. As you follow Bruce and Racinda through their life-changing journey, you will recognize that to be a real success in life, we must first be successful in our homes.

JOHN C. MAXWELL
Founder, The INJOY Group

"For better or for worse, in sickness and in health . . ." We repeat our vows at our wedding like they're poetic clichés from the past, but when those vows are tested, we find out fast how resolved our love really is. *Touching the Shadows* is not just a powerful story of two people's commitment to live out those vows; it's also a clear road map any of us can follow when it's our turn to walk through the valley of the shadow with someone we love.

—DR. TIM KIMMEL
Author of *Little House on the Freeway*

For any couple who has felt more alone sleeping next to each other than they did sleeping single . . . For every husband and wife who have longed to reach across the growing chasm between them, but could not . . . Bruce Nygren expertly walks through secret places of the married heart, ultimately illuminating one of life's greatest mysteries: that pain is often the best path, perhaps the only path, to the rediscovery of true love.

—Becky Freeman
Marriage columnist and author of
Chocolate Chili Pepper Love and *Marriage 911*

If you struggle with God, this book is for you. If you are facing dark days, this book is for you. If you have unanswered questions about suffering, this book is for you. *Touching the Shadows* is a rare glimpse into the authentic faith of two of God's choicest servants. These pages don't offer a Pollyanna approach to life, but instead deliver hope, encouragement, and, most importantly, a real faith in the God who can be trusted. Bruce and Racinda are good friends who have faced some of life's most daunting circumstances. Read this book. You won't regret it.

—Dennis and Barbara Rainey
Executive Director, FamilyLife
Coauthors of *Moments Together for Couples*
and *Starting Your Marriage Right*

Touching the Shadows is a courageous, painful, and redemptive walk through the dark woods of marital and personal agony. Bruce and Racinda honestly and winsomely allow us to see the by-products of selfishness, illness, past abuse, and the normal wear and tear of life, as well as the process of how God redeems us in spite of ourselves. Their story promises that no matter how lost we feel, or how much pain we have experienced, there is hope as we experience God as our wild lover. This is a glorious book.

—DR. DAN ALLENDER
Author of *The Wounded Heart* and *The Healing Path*

Piercingly honest. Painfully confrontational. Impeccably written. *Touching the Shadows* will jolt you into evaluating your personal relationships. With descriptive wording that makes the reader touch, feel, and taste the agony, anger, struggle, and pain of a marriage that is disintegrating, Bruce Nygren offers hope to all of us who have, at times, failed in our relationships. This book is particularly helpful to married couples, but its applications go far beyond marriage. If you long for intimacy, oneness, connectedness, and spiritual unity with the people you are closest to, this book is for you!

—CAROL KENT
President, Speak Up Speaker Services
Author of *Becoming a Woman of Influence*

Faced with the sobering reality that death might very well separate him from his wife, Racinda, Nygren fought hard against waves of despair. The couple had already endured an agonizing distant marriage, offering little preparation for Racinda's terrifying diagnosis of breast cancer. Nygren, eyes wide open, understood and embraced the painful rebirth of his love for Racinda, and watched helplessly as his wife suffered brutal cancer treatments and clung to slender threads of hope. Nygren calls upon his adept literary skills to carefully craft this amazing story of marital renewal during one of life's most horrendous scenarios.

—*PUBLISHERS WEEKLY,*
13 November 2000

Touching *the* Shadows

Touching *the* Shadows

A Love Tested and Renewed

Bruce Nygren

THOMAS NELSON PUBLISHERS
Nashville

Published by Thomas Nelson, Inc., in association with the literary agency
of Alive Communications, 7680 Goddard St., Suite 200, Colorado Springs,
CO 80920.

Library of Congress Cataloging-in-Publication Data

Nygren, Bruce
     Touching the shadows : a love tested and renewed / Bruce Nygren.
         p. cm.
     ISBN 0-7852-6780-8 (hc)
     1. Nygren, Racinda—Health. 2. Nygren, Bruce. 3. Breast—Cancer—
Patients—United States—Biography. 4. Breast—Cancer—Patients—
United States—Family relationships. I. Title
     RC280.B8 N947 2000
     362.1'9699449'0092—dc21
     [B]

                                                              00-045228
                                                              CIP

                    Printed in the United States of America
              1 2 3 4 5 6 7 8 9 10 BVG 05 04 03 02 01 00

Contents

Contents

For Racinda

1

The Moment

March 1997

I KNOW NOW IT WAS THE WEEKEND that changed everything.

Saturday morning began like hundreds of others. With the alarm clock gagged, how satisfying it is to tell your mind to forget weekday worries and drift again into the temporary death of sleep. But this time the little thinker was being a jerk, awake at the dawn's early light, banging the door on the brain closet with the hope of dragging out forgotten ideas, wounds in need of a lick, things to do, unclassified feelings, wrongs to right, postponed pleasures—a heap of stuff so large that not even Saturday's mental fog could conceal it.

And this crazy basketball game! Why had I agreed so willingly to present myself for public humiliation? I was going to coach a basketball game—probably my son's last game ever!

But looming above petty thoughts and anxieties was the state of my mate. Our marriage was sick again, and for the first time I was really scared about us. Always before there had been

1

hopeful relational prescriptions—slick words, flowers, some new household toy, a baby, a vacation, a know-it-all marriage book, a wise counselor, church work, a marriage seminar, a new house—all distractions to dull reality. Not so now. Many months of her roller-coaster moods had left me tired. And more than a little angry.

She lay beside me, but just how far apart were we these days? Groaning feebly, she shifted and rolled on her back, her shoulder now touching mine. In dawn's faint glow, I watched our covering sheet rise and fall in tiny waves, the ebb and flow of her breath. She slept now, but I wondered if the demons of the night had tormented her again.

The first signs had shown months earlier, leaves rattled by a breeze threatening to become a gale. Her body would warm and cool for no apparent reason. More troubling was a slow darkening of her mood, but her annual doctor's checkup yielded no clues. Irritations wormed holes in her resilient outlook, and our normal relational bumping now bore sores. I had reemerged as the provocateur of her pain.

As the weeks passed she had slipped lower on a slope that fell away into a dark canyon. I would try to reach her, flinging ropes woven from hopeful words and deeds, but all snapped or slipped her grasp, none able to bear the weight and halt her slide. The night brought agony, the sweet renewal of sleep replaced by mental overtime, a ceaseless sifting of memories and feelings. Each day she edged nearer exhaustion.

Angry words darted between us. By last month a smog had

swallowed all but familiar landmarks in our relationship. My wife of these many years was convinced that no one cared anymore, not even me. All she could see were the cold, stone, steep walls of her abyss.

Sometimes during a late night's dispute, she would leave the bedroom and flee to a distant corner of the house, far from me, to find shelter from more pain. I would search and find her, but unlike in the past, now I could not always coax her back to our bed.

And there was the grim day, her solitary confinement bleak, when she stunned me by saying, "When I leave this marriage . . ." as though she knew the ending to our story. I let the hurtful words fall, refusing to receive their meaning, but I knew something was dreadfully wrong.

To relieve her sleeplessness our family doctor prescribed pills, which helped only little. We went again to see him, and I did most of the talking. She was so weary that she feared forgetting to tell all the symptoms.

The doctor concluded that the emotional tremors signaled the quake of menopause, which a blood test confirmed. He thought estrogen might alleviate symptoms, level out moods, bring sleep. So more pills were tried and brought some relief. But she wasn't getting better fast enough to suit me. I was mad at her for having problems that stood in the way of my happiness. And over time my seeds of self-pity had sprouted a tree of resentment. Resisting the urge to roll against her body and let the warmth wash over me, perhaps to find another hour of sleep, I slipped quietly from the warm cocoon, and with palpable unease, left to meet the day.

My wife arose tired, weary to the bone after another night of hard work in search of sleep. She was not pleasant, her reserves of charm and goodwill depleted. A wiser man would have left his house. After all, this was Saturday—over the years our preferred day for marital tongue fights. But I was looking for something, a reason to justify dumping my tub of bad feelings. I needed a dog to kick. This memory sickens me.

The argument started over this monumental, life-changing event—*the basketball game.* Our son, age fifteen, was nearing the end of his hoops career. If the team lost this game in their recreational league tournament, the season—basketball—was over. I had been asked at the last minute to substitute for the coach, another team dad who had a schedule conflict. I like basketball, but I'm no coach. The prospect of contributing to the end of organized basketball for my son, something I desperately did not want, stirred my middle-aged, sports-obsessed, American male soul into a lumpy, gurgling stew of sadness, fear, and loss.

My son's mother had made a serious misstep, deciding because of fatigue and low spirits, to spend a quiet morning at home where she would not have to act excited about uncoordinated teenage boys in baggy shorts chasing a round ball under the direction of screaming, overweight, flushed middleaged men.

All of this seemed important to me on this particular day, important enough to trot out my pet grudge and let the brute chew on my mate's tender heart. I made a bad choice related to my anger and went on a sin binge.

"Why aren't you going today, to help me with the game?" I asked her. We were alone in the basement of our home.

"You didn't ask me! And I have so much to do here." Her voice squeaked, tight with tension and fatigue.

"Well, what's *really* important to you? This is his last game!" My words were daggers of accusation.

"Now *wait* a minute!" she countered. "I've been to most of them! Why are you dumping on me like this?"

"I'm not dumping on you! I'm just sick and tired of the way you are acting," I spat. "You don't care about the rest of us. You're just stuck on your own problems."

"What do you mean, I don't care? I've practically given up my life for all of you—I'm dying on the inside!"

Two hurting lovers firing their guns, the accumulated fear, pain, and anger falling as hot metal rain, shrapnel gouging deep.

Tears rolled from her eyes; she turned and ran up the stairs.

There is a word that describes well this anger-fueled assault of another person bearing God's image, a violation not of body, but of soul: *rape*.

As we had countless times before, with the emotional bleeders stanched by pressing family obligations, we climbed in the car—father, mother, son—Family of the Clenched Jaw, and drove wordlessly in our sedan through the streets of suburban sweetness.

And in the heart of me I shed a torrent of tears and mourned my depravity, the wickedness that crouches near every door. I wanted to scream, "I have been a fool! Oh, if I could only take back all of the words and the hate and the acid from my rotting tongue!" But the damage was done, and I was left alone with agonized thoughts: *Just what is happening to us? Is this the time she will say, "I've had enough of this and enough of you!"? Have I finally sabotaged my life's most precious experience—our love, our family? God help me!*

Help was on the way, but not as I envisioned. Hidden in shadows an evil intruder lurked, poised to ravage our smug comfort. But in a horrible, yet beautiful irony, this visitor, intent on destruction, was destined to become just another servant in love's employ.

At the gym I knew my only hope of contributing to victory was to inflame the boys with winning passion in the pre-game huddle. I used some of the best sports clichés: "Leave it all on the floor." "Play this game as if it's your last." "There's no *I* in team!" Blah, blah, blah! The young men listened dutifully and showed stirrings of motivation, but then the game started and hope vanished. As I yelled encouragement and game-turning gems like "GET THAT BALL!" I glanced nervously at the woman sitting across the floor in the top row, eyes ahead, arms folded. Was that a vapor of steam rising from her head?

With the game lost but my coaching ordeal complete, my mood rebounded. Yet blood still oozed from the bandages of my wounded mate. A planned outing to a car show with my son and a friend was next on my agenda. Before leaving with the boys, I gave her a spiritless sentence of regret and a limp hug. She didn't respond.

When I returned later that afternoon, we had crisp but civil conversation, stitching each other up warily. By bedtime the bandages came off. Our marriage was blessed with amazing powers of self-healing. But how many more explosions could we survive? And why was the peace we'd won after twenty years of negotiations again at risk? Had guerrillas infiltrated and found hideouts in some untamed wilderness of our common heart? We fell asleep that night shoulder to shoulder, foxhole partners, our bodies still tense with battlefield adrenaline.

The following day, Sunday, we attended church and dined on potluck lunch with friends. With wounds mending, memory of the battle faded. By nightfall the ice in our words had melted and smiles were less forced. She and I crawled into bed early, eager to enter a night that promised rest in a bed drained of tension. We nestled close and read for a few minutes. My eyelids jerked open and shut as I sagged toward sleep.

Abruptly she laid her book aside and moved a hand and fingers in a circular probe of her breast. She took my hand and pressed it into the soft flesh.

"Do you feel that? I have a lump."

And from that moment life would never be the same.

2

Converging Lines

Earlier Days

I IMAGINE WHAT SURELY MUST HAVE HAPPENED the fall night we exchanged vows.

As we drove west toward hotel sheets, our wedded bodies weary but awake with longing, a vaporous van pulled up to the duplex on Thirty-first Street that was now our home. An anonymous, unseen crew carried the invisible precious cargo into the deserted rooms. Wordlessly the technicians unpacked boxes from piles marked "his" and "hers."

These items, handiwork years in the making and dusty from disuse, must now after the wooing of courtship reappear to decorate a marriage: habits, pet ideas, bad grammar, acid memories, adolescent shames, family customs, appetites, dark looks, odors and oddities, fears, attitudes, flaws, favored sins. All would await us at honeymoon's end.

In her pile, a box of gleaming cutlery, looks good for sharp cutting.

In my stack, a box brimming with vocabulary, words good for angry controlling.

✑

From childhoods come clues found nowhere else.

That I was something of a boiling teapot was long disguised by red cheeks and a shy grin. A loved but unplanned—"Holy-moley-I-thought-I-was-too-old-to-get-pregnant!"—child, I baby-boomed in on the Ides of March, eager for Mother's breast, a blizzard filling the sky, the wind wailing through gaps in ice-crusted windows. I came home in rolls of blankets to a simple prairie house, my infancy disrupting a long-settled family space filled by three older brothers.

I grew on the Dakota plains where all horizons touched a sea of grain. For a boy the rural life enchanted—one day after another of sounds, odors, and sights that stirred the senses. In the barn tiny pigs were born, their afterbirth steaming in the crisp air, the sow wallowing on her side, nudging the offspring to her teats with wet snout, squealing from a too vigorous suck, the air ripe with puddled urine and pods of excrement.

In the house, Mother pulled fresh-baked bread from the oven and served up bowls of potatoes freshly dug, roasted beef, and gravy.

My father, a man of good heart, bore with quiet courage his pain of losing a dad to death while still a boy, as well as the disappointments and indignities of surviving the Great Depression.

We seldom saw the map to Dad's emotional life. Like so many men of his generation, you guessed at what the man felt and had to work with signals and cues, not hard data.

I only knew this instinctively on that summer afternoon when I was about five. As children do, I explored and experimented with the plentiful stuff of the farm. One enticing object was a fifty-gallon drum of motor oil, stored on its side on a wooden stand. A spigot allowed my dad to drain oil out for tractors, the truck, and other uses.

I did manipulate the spigot that sunny day, but I don't remember leaving the valve open. My life was so full of wonder that I probably moved to the next adventure without noticing the black liquid pooling on the ground.

Two hours later I was playing near our house when Father burst through a door and swooped me up, scaring me with his anger-torn face and hot words. I had no idea what was happening and lapsed into a child's terror. I soon found out the nature of my criminal deed as I was lifted and carried swiftly to the scene. Standing next to the large dark stain in the dirt, I learned how precious oil must be, certainly of more value than my crumbling innocence. The little boy did not understand why ignorance deserved such fury.

I received my punishment with tears. As a bonus I had a lesson in anger, a sweet taste of the self-pity nectar, spiked with a shot of hard stuff—indignant rage. But what really can a five-year-old do with intoxicating juice like that? Swallow.

This is not to suggest that little boys aren't depraved agents capable of bad acts that deserve correction, including some butt percussion. But on that memorable day I learned too much about how this fallen planet is populated with bruised hearts. I learned how big people often relieve themselves of frustration on the small or weak. I learned that the ones you love sometimes do hateful things. I learned that a safe world can fill suddenly with danger. I learned that anger, streaking like lightning from a flicking tongue, can kill without leaving a drop of blood.

This is not a victim's lament. I don't blame every personal pothole since age five on my fuming daddy, whom I love more each year because now I know better how tenuous everyone's goodness is. I do know, though, how even our smallest sins carry enough potential evil to scar a life.

Four hundred miles south of my prairie outpost, a baby girl was born in Iowa, the second daughter for a couple who raised cattle and corn on a half section of rich dirt.

Growing up in a family with no brothers, she had abundant opportunity—in an era before feminist outrage—to move beyond playing school on the porch with her sister, tending dolls, and mastering inside chores. By necessity and with obvious aptitude, she gravitated toward doing the outdoor chores traditionally assigned to boys.

She liked this, tagging behind her father whose daily tasks covered an exhilarating spectrum of encounters with beasts and machines. Something was always birthing, grinding, snorting, backfiring, mooing, gurgling, smoking, dying—a daily interactive experience that would shame any zoo or museum.

Of course there were requirements. In spite of her busy farmhand schedule, a young lady was required to master tap dance and ballet, as well as piano lessons. But the older she grew and the more adept she became at handling both the four-legged critters and the four-wheeled machines, the less was seen of her tending laundry and stove.

With her father's purebred Angus cow herd producing champion calves, the girl joined her local 4-H club to learn how to groom a young steer, to shampoo the hide and twist and comb the tail. She also studied the strategies of leading the animal around the show ring at local fairs, urging the beast with a pointed prod to present its relevant parts fetchingly to judges wearing cowboy hats and wrinkled brows, sucking on toothpicks or cigarettes.

The days and seasons passed, a graceful rhythm meted by sky, earth, and beast. A railroad line split the farm, and at all hours of day and night the sounds of diesel engine, locomotive horn, clashing metal, and groaning wheels gave the farm's life a discordant background music.

On Christmas Eve the family drove to Grandpa's for a traditional choice of chili or oyster soup (no one wanted to risk ruining Christmas by eating both). Summer delights were a July Fourth picnic with kin and a quick vacation via car to marvel at Colorado peaks. But life, mainly for such farmers, was the farm.

Near her tenth birthday the girl arrived home from school, and around the house ran a puppy, greeting her with leaps and licks. The Australian blue shepherd, a birthday present from Mom and Dad, had arrived earlier by train from Colorado.

The dog and the girl bonded in an instant, and because of the pup's long journey on the rails, she named him Hobo.

When I was about eight, my brother nearest in age left to serve in the army. Although I had a playmate or two on nearby farms, increasingly my companions were ragged mixed-breed farm dogs, barnyard cats, bunnies caught in the trees of shelter breaks, and my father, who each year expanded my role as his chief assistant in caring for the animals and raising the crops.

Living in a rural area so unpopulated that a rifle shot fired from our front door might not reach the nearest neighbor's house, I acquired a taste for space. When not farm-handing for Dad, I was free to wander with the dog the hundreds of acres, smelling the turned dirt, the blooming alfalfa, the slime fermenting in a slough. With the wind a gale, I would lie flat against the earth in the tall grass and watch the sky and think and dream. Is it possible to think too much? I think so.

One of those years my thoughts, assisted by a horde of blissful new sensations, turned to girls. My portage from boy to man might have required less sweat and stumbling if I'd had a sister, a female cousin my age who lived nearby, or a few more girl playmates. To me girls were mysterious, distant, unattainable creatures who lived in a foreign world to which I held no visa. If a sister had shared the farm, belching over oatmeal, leaving her grimy underpants on the stairway, and edgy amid her monthly woe, I would have exchanged some romantic daydreams for reality.

My fantasies were not of sex. At this age such an encounter between two bodies seemed impossible, even frightening—*You would have to take off your clothes in front of a* girl? Plus I had seen the sex act demonstrated numerous times by the dogs, cats, and sheep roaming the farm. If this was sex—forget it. Who would want to participate in anything resembling all of that weird bashing, "baa-aa-ing," and bumping I saw under a cloud of dust in the barnyard? I was more than content to stick with my musings of just being near a girl in some warm, friendly way.

During her childhood music was just an activity for the girl in Iowa, but as she grew it became a precious soul mate, available when needed to soothe some tender spots in her passionate heart.

Entering high school and busy, the girl-becoming-young-woman no longer eagerly followed Father's footprints around the farm and was seen less frequently where doors slammed and suppers were silent. Life changes, and some memories bring tears but no explanation.

Her dream was to sing, which she did in choirs at school and church, but she was so deft with the keyboard that much of her music time was spent accompanying others during vocal and instrumental competitions. And she also played piano for the high school boys' choir—not bad duty for a spirited young woman.

Her desire for music was so palpable that the band director recruited her from the crowd to become his drum major for the marching band, a task so welcome that she immediately grasped the whistle between her teeth and never looked back.

When she turned sixteen and received her license to date from her parents, another musician, a drummer, asked her to be his friend and also to join a band. So off they went on dates, suitably costumed, to play in a Dixieland band at service club gigs.

The girl on piano didn't care much for the fumes from smoke and booze, but even tinkling some Dixie was making music. The melodies and beat were an escape, a drowning out of a noise only she could hear, a sound like the crash of a delicate and tender vase, tipped clumsily, shattering to a thousand bits on a hard floor, a spill of glass with no promise of repair.

✑

My mixture of fear and awe concerning girls did not abate until college. Now I was playing in real relationship games, but powered still by those romantic longings fine-tuned while gazing for hours at the sky, I sought a perfect woman who would magically fill all the empty spots in my soul. To these lovely, perfectly human coeds I dated, I must have seemed discontent, a restless explorer, peering with wild eyes beyond the moment to some hazy, enticing horizon.

I graduated from college in 1969 and immediately entered the U.S. Army. The Vietnam War raged in full fury, in Vietnam and in America. I was not anti-war but definitely pro-life—mine. So I enlisted for training as a particular type of intelligence specialist, a job my recruiter told me would most likely station me on American soil or in Europe.

After completing all of my basic and intelligence training, I received orders to report to a military language school located in El Paso, Texas, to study Vietnamese. I now had a clear idea of the location of my next assignment.

The language training lasted nearly a year. We young soldiers found our own unique ways to deal with the likelihood that in a matter of months we would fly away to join a hated war. Most everyone lived at some degree of excess, storing up experiences and sensations that the war might maim or kill. Some of the soldiers with girlfriends back home rushed ahead with plans and married. Others just chased and chased, hoping to find a memory to hold during coming dark, uncertain days.

A friend introduced me to a nurse, a girl from a large Roman Catholic family who had enlisted in the army as a way to finance her college education. We hit it off, and before long my time away from the numbing recitation of Vietnamese phrases was spent with her.

Eventually we both ended up in Vietnam and on rare occasions I visited her at a medevac hospital. After her twelve-hour shifts in an intensive care ward, we strolled about the compound, looking beyond the concertina wire perimeter at the Pacific surf shooting spray into the moonlight.

We listened to music and talked of what might be when the war for us was over. She shipped home and months later I followed. We had survived, but though we tried to rehab our wartime friendship, the relationship had no lasting peacetime purpose.

We said good-byes and I watched her leave. Some things just can't be. I'd tasted a closeness long pursued, but it was just a prelude, a harbinger of the destined love, waiting for me now, just around the bend.

In her high-school years, the young woman in Iowa discovered that her passion must become her life, so she left in the fall of 1970 to study music at a small liberal arts college. And when this music department thwarted her dream of singing, urging her in a familiar reprise to stay at the keyboard, she transferred to the large state university, where she double-majored in voice and piano.

But before leaving the small college, she had a wonderful but strange visitation for someone who had grown up near the altar of an organized Protestant religion. Friends invited her to a Sunday evening meeting at a Catholic church, and while guitars played and a priest or two watched bemusedly from the sidelines, some "lay brothers and sisters" explained the really good news about the best Man this woman would ever meet.

And for the first time she heard that faith was more and much better than church; it could be a one-on-one adventure with this great Man and Deity whose name for good or ill lived on many lips—Jesus. And so began a most intriguing friendship.

So she said yes to such an obviously beneficial relationship, a no-brainer long before the world discovered no-brainers. And as a part of this new day with sins and stains freshly removed just for the asking, she eagerly washed away the stains of others, too, in the cleansing stream of forgiveness.

It was good that the woman had this Jesus in her life, because she had concluded after some disappointments that the man-woman career might not interest her. But she did leave herself an out, commenting once to her new Friend in a not-too-holy-sounding prayer, "If a man is going to get anywhere with me, he will have to fight through this wall I'm putting up to keep the ones with lusting hands away."

After graduate school I moved to Des Moines, Iowa, to unwind the next reel of my life. I started work at the city's daily newspaper, found an efficiency apartment, and began looking for a way to forget that wartime romance.

My first Sunday in the city, I attended a large church and learned that male voices were needed for programs during the coming holiday season. Alone in a new city and eager to sing, I went that afternoon to the rehearsal. A young woman was directing the choir, taking the place on this particular day—I learned—of the choir director who was away.

I found a spot with other bass singers in the back row, and over the top of my music book, watched the young director's hands inscribe the music in delicate arcs. I had no idea that our lives would some day entangle in the most magical and mundane ways, that together we would make love and sometimes hate, and from our bodies would come more eternal souls to bear the eternal image. And that during a much distant time the searing heat of a fearful moment would finally forge a lasting love.

No, on that soft fall afternoon, with the dipping sun backlighting the trees in a dull orange, I was just another boy searching for the other half of his life, wondering what the girl's name was, and if this one shaping the music with such passionate hands had a boyfriend.

3

Joined

September 1974

HER NAME WAS RACINDA, a homemade name constructed by parents looking for a pleasing *R* name to match an older sister's Roberta. And she didn't have a boyfriend, but her heartthrob was music, an alluring suitor.

While warbling bass and eyeing the assistant director, I thought at times Racinda's green eyes warmed when meeting mine. But if the two of us were any music to make, the tune was only in the mind of the composer.

Other women were more interested, so I fumbled through one relationship after another. My dating game now spanned a decade, and like some ancient quarterback with his head rung like a cathedral bell, I knew this career needed to end. I'd flung so many passes I could barely lift my arm.

I had never forgotten the magical days of yore when older brothers Dick, Irv, and Burt had brought home their brides-to-be—in my fantasy factory they had seemed princesses of some distant kingdom. Long ago they all had bestowed grandchildren. But here I was, a senior single nearing the scandalous age of thirty with nary a prospect in sight. My mother had sewn a quilt for the marriage bed of each son. One day, in resignation and without ceremony, she handed my quilt to me. Even this intimate of God was exhausted in her prayers that her baby son would ever marry.

Desperation was upon me, too. How could it be, with others coupling with the apparent ease of rabbits, that any man so eager to nest and father children could struggle so to strike a match?

In spring of 1975, after another failed relationship, I called Racinda. This was a suicidal leap off the relational cliffs because the girl showed no interest in me. She said yes—but with a novel contingency. The night of our date she was "babysitting" a sixth-grade boy. Could he come along? *This is shaping up to be an evening of heart-stopping romance,* I thought. My skepticism was rewarded. Our trio watched a basketball game with the little guy parked right there between us. Since he had to go to bed at nine, the evening ended early for everyone. No need to call Mother just yet.

Not discouraged easily, like a salmon battling upstream to the breeding waters, I tried one more date. Minus our pre-adolescent chaperone (Was he busy with a date of his own?), we attended a lecture. No magic. No sparks. No smoke. No nothing. No future.

Racinda plunged back into her music, and I just plunged.

We stayed lightly in touch, small-talking at choir rehearsals. Months passed. A friend asked me to double-date to a concert on New Year's Eve, and I thought again of the music woman—aha! *Wouldn't she like a music thing?* But this seemed a fool's errand. She just wasn't interested. Now I know that her diffidence made her mysterious and alluring. She said yes.

This time—fire. On a cold night the music charmed us, and we laughed in the early morning while eating the New Year's first meal. We parted late from our friends, and then at Racinda's apartment, shared hot tea and talked until dawn. When two souls align, there's catching up to do.

After the sun had well lit the new day, standing wearily by her door, I took her in my arms. Too tired for more words, she laid her head on my chest, as though finding refuge. Moments later I drove away but never really left.

When I asked Racinda to drive with me on Memorial Day weekend to meet my parents, I was near the conclusion that we should marry. But my intent was top secret, locked away in my stoic Swede emotional vault.

As we motored north through the endless infant corn and bean fields in Iowa and Minnesota, we talked and held happy hands, overflowing with the backlog of news and intimate tidbits accumulated since a similar conversation the night before. We thought we knew everything about each other—until together again when we found new veins of information lode. Lovers make the best students.

After five months of such discovery, I now had a grasp on the details of her life. I could decide Racinda should be my wife. This was a good thing, but I really didn't know her that well. When it comes to love, the lovers make a down payment of disclosure to each other, promising to pay off any knowledge due on an installment plan. It's the Maker's system of joining hearts, and it works well, although with interesting twists.

As we drove around the Twin Cities, I explained how my parents, both children of Swedish immigrants, had met, married, and raised their family—except for me—in Minneapolis and St. Paul. Then after the life on the North Dakota frontier for twenty-plus years, Mom and Dad had retired by a river, where Dad now fished summer and winter.

Three hours later we arrived home and were met at the door by Mother, her face flushed red with anticipation, hands fingering the folds in her apron. Father stood back, smiling, his presentation controlled in the Scandinavian way.

After hellos, fumbling hugs, and Mom's sloppy neck kisses, we brought Racinda and her bag to the guest room. Always angling for the laugh, Mom said with twinkle, giggle, and blush, "I sure wish we could put you two up here together, but not just yet!" *Oh yes; you're not the only one, Ma.*

Our days of Minnesota spring, the air warm and tinged with scents of awakening pine and earth reborn, were harmony. Racinda and I walked sandy trails through the tall trees and ate

Mom's homemade bread and meat-and-potato casseroles. With Dad we fished for sunfish and crappies, the river's water—not long since ice—chilling the sides of the aluminum boat. One afternoon I paddled Racinda downstream in a canoe.

Once I cornered Father and asked to go to the local bank to retrieve some savings bonds from my military life, a cash reserve awaiting a special expense. Racinda overheard and with intuition knew what I knew—soon one less ring would gleam in a Des Moines jewelry store.

Three weeks later on her birthday, June 22, I had her fish in my pocket, where she caught gold and stone, and I asked the most important question anyone ever asks. And she answered yes.

We married the next November 6. Mother's quilt finally had its marriage bed.

The night our bodies and hearts finally merged into one, I had no hint or care about the insurgency forming inside one of Racinda's breasts. And if I had known an evil enemy would someday invade our sweet joy, it would have made no difference. Isn't that love's wonder—its weightless optimism no matter what threat of heaviness life might drape on its broad shoulders? In the honeymoon season, love is not blind, just mercifully nearsighted.

Racinda and I had attended pre-marital counseling. Although the man discerned our sharp edges that would in time cut and draw blood, we were inhaling romantic helium, soaring above the petty and mundane that might snag and crash other couples.

To its credit, love is an inept prosecutor. It may trip over smoking-gun evidence the size of a howitzer but never ask the hard questions. I'd mastered the facts of Racinda's life before our merger, but those details were trivial compared to the point—us. If with some bizarre motive I had interrogated to learn her medical history or the blights of her family tree, I would have received the replies with a smug nod. I had no idea that an armada of radiation had pounded Racinda's baby body, and if she'd told me, I would have considered it more evidence of her need for my healing affection.

When we spoke our vows, there was no blip on my screen that a "worse" would ever compete with the "better." We were generic honeymooners, blissfully one, off to conquer life. And we were right—our love would conquer. It just wasn't to happen the way we dreamed.

We flew to our honeymoon at a tropical resort on the Pacific Coast of Mexico. Along the way the airline lost our bags, so we arrived at the hotel with only what we were wearing, which we quickly shed. If there's ever a time to lose your shirt, the honeymoon is it.

Soon we were into the typical honeymoon routine, long sessions behind closed doors and curtains, interspersed with brief, obligatory forays outside the room—to swim or eat a hurried meal. After two days I became uncomfortably guilty about so much pleasure. Growing up in rural America in the 1950s, my parents and other truth merchants, when pressed, would admit that sex was God's invention, but their body language gave away that they thought it was not one of His better achievements. With such upbringing I, too, could admit that sex was a good part of married life. But this much sex? Years would pass before I would know that it wasn't sex that unsettled me, but rather the emotional nakedness required.

Alarmed by intimacy's spotlight, I sought to control our script. My own desire to hide peaked out, and to cover myself, I began the process of reshaping my fiery mate into a less threatening companion. This certainly is a dark side of marriage, the selfish and subtle agenda to refashion a person God created into one more in line with our wishes. Every person does have flaws in attitudes and behavior, but why do we take saw and sandpaper to remodel the essence of another divinely crafted human being? Would we want to improve the texture of a rose petal with a grinder? But we think nothing of putting the rasp to the "rough spots" of one we love most.

So I dug through my mental ragbag for a reason to curtail all this excessive undressing—"We need to do some sight-seeing while we're here!" was one that sounded noble.

So one day we rode in a boat and snorkeled in a bay nearby,

and we sampled the yummy-smelling dish roasting on a beach grill. By the next day my stomach was knotted. With our seven days, six nights winding down, we returned to Mexico City, where I discovered we were nearly broke. With growling stomach and just enough pesos to fetch a cab to the airport, we flew home to Iowa to get on with our marriage. The honeymoon was over. My stomach and I were both relieved.

Settling into a normal routine brought comfort. Racinda continued her music work at the church, and I rode the bus downtown each morning to a newspaper job. Our home was an old duplex furnished with the basics—table, chairs, couch, bed. We had our newlywed skirmishes followed by awesome reconciliations. Mainly we enjoyed being mister and missus. At night we watched TV or played Ping-Pong or went for walks. Most of the time we went to bed early, then after some marital aerobics, beelined to the kitchen for a goodnight snack—certainly the tastiest meal of the day.

I accepted a new job in Nashville, Tennessee, and nine months after the wedding, we moved and started afresh. Now we were alone with some time on our hands, hundreds of miles away from family and old friends. We drew closer, exploring a new place, sailing, tennis, more walks. On Saturday nights we crawled into bed and watched *Gunsmoke* reruns on our twelve-inch black-and-white TV, not caring the least that the mighty Matt Dillon looked the size of an armed finger puppet inside the tiny box. None of that mattered; we were together and much in love.

By spring of the following year, Racinda was pregnant. With more room needed for the baby on the way, I claimed my GI rights and we purchased a home, a small brick rancher costing a whopping $37,500. Weeks later we traded cars—just like that, the Celica coupe I considered standard equipment for my single life was replaced by a *station wagon*. Gee whiz, all we needed to complete our middle-class utopia was a dog!

Our life filled with the activity that accompanies jobs, house, yard, and expected baby. Not much time now to talk, to walk, to watch TV late and sleep in. Instead of an evening sitting side by side reading, we might rush to the Lamaze class or paint the baby's nursery. Our life together, still in its infancy, subtly began to divide.

We spent Christmas of 1978 alone. Racinda was now too swollen and tired to host company or enjoy a visit to someone else's house. Travel was out of the question. On Christmas Day I took a walk while Racinda rested. I encountered an Irish setter with sad eyes, hungry, no collar. She followed me home and lay down near the back door. At sunset the dog was still there, so I fed her table scraps. At bedtime she'd not moved, so I offered a bunk in the garage. The next day I posted "Dog Found" signs in the neighborhood. No replies. I bought a bag of dog food. We christened her Christie and the adoption was complete. With the dog on board, now all we lacked was the baby.

Noelle was born three days later. During labor we tried

Lamaze gamely—I coached Racinda, noting the time between contractions and helping her pant correctly. But finally the pain overwhelmed and an epidural was ordered. Near midnight the time drew near, and Racinda, nurses, doctor, and I in my gown entered the delivery room. Noelle arrived red, wrinkled, and wet from Mother's womb with Father noting all the basic equipment: face with nose, eyes, mouth, and ears; arms and hands with fingers; little bowed legs with feet and toes; a heavy mat of black hair. Her lungs inflated and she squealed. Yes!

A nurse wrapped Noelle in a blanket and took her for a bath and exam. I squeezed Racinda's hand and wiped the sweat of hard labor from her brow. The doctor led me into a side room, and knowing of my faith, asked if we could pray. We knelt shoulder to shoulder beside a bed, and the doctor thanked God for the miracle we'd just witnessed, the gift of a healthy child. My tears flowed, full and hot, a moment of *crescendo,* the years of longing over. At last I had a family of my own.

We brought Noelle home two days later, my joy mixed with terror. She was so small and looked so fragile. What if her tiny heart stopped? What if she wouldn't eat? When she cried, what did that mean? What, exactly, were we to do with this little creature?

At the hospital the nurses had shown me how to hold her and support her neck so her head wouldn't flop, but my hands felt as maneuverable as steam shovels. Taking no risks, when

I needed to pick her up, I leaned close, tucked in all dangling body parts, and crushed the baby to my chest—like a fullback clutching a football with both hands and arms, afraid of fumbling in the lunge over the goal line.

We learned that Noelle was still on the time zone she'd established in the womb—sleep by day, party at night. We tried our tricks (not many) to induce sleep. Her eyes finally would shut and after easing her into the crib, we sprinted for our bedroom, desperate for rest. In minutes we'd hear the tiny whimper, leap from bed to mount the rescue, and start the whole process again. Those first nights, even while asleep, our bodies were rigid with tension, our ears calibrated to catch the smallest noise.

Racinda was nursing Noelle, or so we hoped. We worried that our baby wasn't getting enough food—were we inadvertently starving the child? Would we end up in jail?

Who should we call? Our parenting seemed clumsy and stupid. A friend, who was a nurse and mom herself, came to share insights and skills. Noelle soon ate and slept better. She cried less, too, apparently gaining confidence that these two large humans with anxious expressions and tired eyes might actually work out.

During the times—measured often in seconds—when Noelle was full, dry, clean, content, and dressed smartly in a gown with stocking feet, I sat and cradled her in my arms, filled with awe at the majesty of life's cycles. I gazed at the now familiar face, watching her whispery eyelids flutter and her lips form the shape of an *O*. Her eyes sometimes opened in a glaze and appeared to study my face, at her age perceiving what? I twirled the tiny fingers and wiped drips of drool from her lips . . .

On this pilgrim's trek, only so few moments dazzle with intensity—virgin awakenings that turn prairie sod in our souls, leaving memories ever fresh.

On a morning in March, the day before my birthday, the phone rang in my work cubicle. It was one of my brothers, announcing that Mother was direly ill from a stroke.

Hours later, a second call. She was dead.

We flew home, wife, daughter, and me—my family. At funerals of my kin a cousin with a rich bass voice would sing a hymn of Swedish origin, the tune and message a holy ointment:

> *Children of the Heavenly Father*
>
> Children of the heav'nly Father
> Safely in His bosom gather;
> Nestling bird nor star in heaven
> Such a refuge e'er was given.
>
> God His own doth tend and nourish,
> In His holy courts they flourish;
> From all evil things He spares them,
> In His mighty arms He bears them.

Joined

Neither life nor death shall ever
From the Lord His children sever;
Unto them His grace He showeth,
And their sorrows all He knoweth.

Praise the Lord in joyful numbers,
Your Protector never slumbers;
At the will of your Defender
Ev'ry foe-man must surrender.

Though He giveth or He taketh,
God His children ne'er forsaketh;
His the loving purpose solely
To preserve them pure and holy.

Words by Caroline Sandell Berg (1832–1903); translated by Ernst W. Olsen (1870–1958). Text copyright © Board of Publication, Lutheran Church in America. Reprinted by permission of Augsburg Fortress.

We placed Mom in the sandy ground at a pine-filled cemetery near the banks of the same river that flowed by her home.

And on the plane ride back to Nashville, I held Noelle in my lap, glad in my sadness for a world so wonderfully saved that death loses to life.

Sometimes after we put Noelle to bed—bathed, powdered, diapered, fed, and prayed over, I would slip out of the tiny home and roam the hilly streets of our dimly lit neighborhood, welcoming the time alone in the dark, quiet night to reflect on things mundane and profound, and to try to understand the puzzling emptiness in my chest.

I walked a circuit that brought me to a hill where I could see our house below, as well as across the valley to a ridge miles away where lights flickered from homes tucked high on hillsides. I would imagine that between my overlook and the distant heights was a vast inland sea; I could almost hear waves splashing against the shore and the putt-putt of motorboats bringing fishermen in to dock or bearing young lovers out to taste the night.

Why did I feel so restless, so filled with desire to push off from the shore in my own boat and ride out through the breakers toward the distant, mysterious lights?

Now married four years, a husband and father well set, the newness of family life had faded. My mind saw years of domestic toil ahead, and I felt confined. After years of searching for a mate, when each day bore the delicious potential of some new face, I knew Eden's time for seeking bones and flesh like mine was complete. My heart had found its home and had no more need to wander. To look and long now was lust, but I missed the adrenaline high of the adventure. And I grieved.

A shiver from the evening chill would shake my sailing fantasy. Reengaging with reality, I hiked the hill to our hut, to warmth, to the port where a sailor home from sea can weather life's deep waters.

Joined

❦

On vacation our threesome would drive in the wagon north from Tennessee along America's backbone to visit Racinda's home on the Iowa farm. On summer days everyone would rise early to enjoy hearty food, activity in the fields, and visits with neighbors and relatives who stopped by. Noelle was hoisted on shoulders to view the black moo-moos munching cud beyond wood fences. The barn was exotic—steaming dung, buzzing flies, spiders casting nets, rats scrambling for cover, and half-wild kittens fleeing with hiss and spit if anyone drew too near.

Each day's excitement and fresh air left us weary and eager to crawl into the old cotton-soft bed Racinda and I shared upstairs in the farmhouse. As lights died one by one, sleep brought quiet—the only dominant sound a Big Ben clock on the floor below ticktocking the seconds of the night.

One such night Racinda was exhausted from the hard labor of being both the daughter of the past and the wife and mother of the present. After a glancing kiss, wordlessly she turned her back and sank into sleep, like a stone dropped into a pond.

Rays from the moon made relics in the room visible. On a shelf several ancient dolls drooped, misted with dust, long forgotten. Their posture in the half-light seemed to shout, "I'm depressed! No one has even touched me in years!" Through the opening into a small closet I saw a row of dresses, their plastic covers shiny in the moonlight.

Before I submerged in sleep, too, I wondered what the inanimate witnesses could tell of the girl-turned-woman, now buried in sleep beside me. What dreams and tears had warmed this pillow? Did she ever wish for a prince to lead her to dance until dawn stopped the music? Did someone like me ever flash on the screen of her longings?

A breeze rustled the silky curtains, and in the barnyard a calf bawled for its mother's teat. The sound raised a memory Racinda had entrusted to me of her childhood pal, the dog Hobo. More than once, the two of them had sat side by side in an empty manger in that creaking, dusty barn. As Racinda sobbed, the tears of an angry hurt spurting from her eyes, the sweet dog Hobo had rested his head against her shaking side, licking away stray tears with an eager tongue.

In April of 1981 Racinda was pregnant with our number two.

Near the end of the pregnancy, she developed toxemia and spent her final weeks in bed. On January 8 her water broke and Allan was born in the afternoon, a strong body wiggling from the womb. Once again a nurse took the baby and while the doctor finished attending to Racinda, I left the delivery room and waited outside.

Minutes later the nurse came and said words I have learned to dread—"Don't worry but . . ." Then she told me that something was wrong with one of my son's ears. We went to the nursery and she showed me the left side of his head, where it looked like someone had folded his tiny ear over and glued it shut. Trying to calm my anxiety, the nurse said, "That doesn't look like much of a problem—just something a doctor could snip open. When the pediatrician comes, we'll have him take a look."

The doctor came, and after examining Allan, met with us in Racinda's room. He admitted that he had never seen this rare medical condition. Allan had no ear canal and would require surgery to reconstruct an outer ear. The doctor shared what he remembered from medical school—that the baby might have no hearing in his left ear and there might be other complications. Overall, though, Allan's health was solid.

After he left, Racinda and I sat quietly. She was weary from the ordeal of childbirth, and now this sad cloud dampened her relief and joy. We said our prayers and good-byes and I left for home. Waiting in the hall for the elevator, gloom swept through me. Just hours before, like any father my dreams had come true of the little man who would help me relive the escapades and triumphs of boyhood. Visions of games with balls and bats filled my head.

The empty elevator arrived, and I stepped in and pushed the button. As the steel cube dropped to ground level, I realized I was not alone. The elevator was full of the presence of God. He had come to comfort me, to relieve my anxiety and pain. I heard no words but the message was clear: *Don't worry or be afraid. I have special plans for this boy.*

The elevator doors opened on the first floor. I stepped off, still shaken and perplexed, but the horrible fear was gone.

4

Mounting Pressures

Spring 1985

I WAS A MAN IN A HURRY, not always sure where I was going, but determined to get there fast.

There were so many good and urgent things to do. Like most men in their thirties, I was constructing my empire. At work I was eager for promotions and pay raises. At home I had projects—cutting wood, building a dollhouse or toy lawn mower for Christmas, rooting out an overgrown hedge, constructing a sandbox, raising a storage barn to store our abundant stuff.

My ambition and work ethic were good. But my understanding of what it means to provide for your family was too focused on material matters. Like most everybody, my values deck was missing a few cards.

Racinda was stuck in overdrive, too, caring for the children, teaching piano, volunteering at church, studying for a master's degree in conducting.

Above all, we were both consumed by the relentless

demands of caring for small people—feedings, diaper changes, ear infections, baths, teething, potty maneuvers, temper tantrums, paddlings, scraped knees, bedtime stories, and piggyback rides. At the end of most days, the two large people had no energy left to deal with their tantrums or scraped hearts. And seldom time for a bedtime story.

My emotional compass had shifted to less complicated loves—those darling children who yelled out "Daddy" and came running when I beeped the horn in the carport after work.

Even though we ate at the same table, loved the same children, and shared the same bed, Racinda and I were acting a bit more like roommates than lovers.

As my attention divided in many directions, Racinda drifted to her passion for music. Since her teenage years, music had been Racinda's refuge—an island paradise where her soul found lush peace and light. Music set Racinda free, her eyes sparkling and her body taut. This unrestrained, raging joy both enticed and alarmed me; she seemed like a wild horse in full gallop about to drag us both over a precipice.

So I did what is so natural when you fear another's passion: I reined her in.

Not long after Allan's birth, without warning Racinda's heart began beating rapidly, so fast that neither of us could count the pulse. Such incidents were scary but infrequent and lasted just a minute or so. Our family doctor was not concerned.

That was fine with Racinda, who did not care much for seeing doctors. She had too many painful memories of dozens of childhood penicillin shots received for inflamed tonsils. As an adult she considered her health good, except for one nagging fear.

Long before her memory, as a one-month-old, Racinda was gulping from her mother's breast one day when suddenly she stopped, gagged, and struggled to breathe. Her mom slid Racinda upright and gently patted her back. After eternal seconds, the baby inhaled with a gasp and resumed her meal. Several weeks later Racinda again gagged, choked violently, and stopped breathing. Her body went limp and turned blue. Uncertain of what to do, instinctively her mother turned her upside down and patted her back, first gently, then with increasing force. Racinda revived.

A doctor diagnosed the problem as an enlarged thymus pressing against her windpipe. The thymus has as its ordained role the final assembly of T cells, also known as killer cells. These hired guns patrol the body, hunting down and executing bacteria, fungi, viruses, and other harmful organisms. One of their most important missions is to find and liquidate mutant, freak cells—otherwise known as cancer.

The doctor said that a series of X rays should shrink the thymus and end the symptoms. The treatment worked. Racinda no longer coughed, struggled to breathe, or turned blue.

Not many years after Racinda received these doses of radiation, which beamed into the base of her neck and upper chest, the medical community found other ways to treat a wayward thymus and concluded that pouring massive radiation into the malleable cells of a child was not a good idea. Racinda's baby-girl body had billions of blood cells, all striving in orchestrated pandemonium to achieve their intricate harmony of tasks. We know that a wounded cell—and its heirs, crippled in their ability to contribute normally and purposefully—may live, divide, and die in harmless anonymity for years. Is it possible that one or more cells damaged by radiation hibernated, masqueraded, acclimated? Did some twisted angry ones flee through the red streams to caves and wait—hoarding their ammunition until the day of revolution? Was a compromised thymus not as able to train the commandos to go find and destroy them?

Racinda's mother was told—later—that her daughter for the rest of her life should always tell her doctors about these radiation treatments, which medical research had in time revealed would increase her risk of thyroid cancer.

So Racinda told her doctors . . . and now and then on her own probed her neck area for suspicious swelling. But nothing ever came of it.

Although I was falling out of sync as a husband, I found my rhythm as a daddy. The world of children I understood: You eat, run around a lot, and when you get tired you find someone's lap and sleep. If you skin your knee, you cry and a nice big person will kiss and hug away your wound.

I relished it all—holding the little hands on walks, the

splashing and giggles in the bathtub, the sweet smell of sweat on a toddler's neck.

Nearly every night, in the waning minutes before their early bedtimes, the three of us would tumble. I played many roles, but our favorite was Horse. I was not a well-behaved pony. Noelle and Allan would lock me in my stall, then turn in for the night. As soon as all was quiet, bad Horse always escaped, and with much whinnying and clomping, led his shrieking caretakers on wild chases.

But as much fun as we had on normal days, vacations were our best playtimes, unimpeded by interruptions from my chores in the adult world.

Once in late fall we loaded our small wagon and drove to Gulf Shores, Alabama, for a week's stay on the Gulf of Mexico. The rental house stood on stilts at the end of a long sandbar; with summer residents long gone, the miles of sand and water were ours alone.

The first night it rained and the clouds hung low like dark drapes. The wind blew, and just yards from our door, waves slammed the shore. We read books, said our prayers, and went to bed early. Only days before, a hurricane had surged a high tide underneath this house. The sounds of threatening weather filled the night, and in an uneasy sleep I wondered if we would awaken surrounded by water, cut off from the mainland.

Morning came gray and moist, but our lodging remained high and dry. With no possibility of beach time, we drove to Mobile for sight-seeing. We returned that afternoon, and while

Racinda and Noelle hunted shells, I watched Allan finish a nap. After mother and daughter came back, Allan awakened and he and I went exploring. At dusk the overcast sky cracked—just a sliver—in the west, and the red of the setting sun backlit a distant oil rig in the gulf.

I turned from this sky fire toward our beach house. Against the blackening night the lights from our rented bungalow twinkled bright and warm. With the surf roar drowning other sounds, Allan and I could see Racinda and Noelle through a large window, moving as though in pantomime on a giant screen, setting the table for dinner.

My eyes misted, my chest filling with such sweet longing. This vision was a realization of dreams, for in that cabin filled with warmth and the aroma of bubbling stew, I saw the completion of a lifetime search for love, safety, and belonging.

Chilled, hungry, and damp, Allan and I walked hand in hand from the blackness to the light . . . to home.

Racinda was the first to grow weary of our festering relational pain, even though initially she believed her discomfort had few links to me. She found a woman counselor, and after a visit or two gently informed me that the sage would love for me to come along sometime for a joint visit.

I was not interested. I was the jut-jawed builder, moving fast and purposefully on my construction projects. As an editor (i.e., builder) of books, I knew enough—thank you—about how counselors assisted other weak and flawed souls. My operative assessment of people with problems was: *Pity, pity, pity. Thank God for the blessing of my ox-like emotional health!*

So I wasn't just displeased that my wife was talking to a counselor, I was offended. This dysfunctional crud shouldn't happen here in my family. *Could this reflect poorly on me? If others found out, would they think I was somehow responsible?*

But I had a dilemma. Since I viewed myself as a sensitive 1980s kind of guy, outwardly I supported Racinda's quest to fix *her* problems—assuming that in a few sessions the cure would be complete and life would once again be rosy.

After avoiding the joint session as long as possible, I finally went slinking in. I fabricated a reason to be absent from my office and hoped no one I knew would see my car in the counselor's parking lot and draw embarrassing conclusions.

Racinda and the counselor welcomed me with smiles. The room was well lit and had a business feel; I was relieved, no dimmed lights, candles, incense. And there were chairs to sit on—not a couch in sight. After some introductory chitchat in which I made clear how I had edited books written by well-known psychologists (Translation: "A well-versed, together kind of man like me doesn't need to be here, but—hey—I'm big, I want to support my hurting wife"), we began discussing my perceptions of Racinda's background and experiences—how they related to her current jumble of feelings. I rambled on, warming to the task, dishing out one insightful comment after another to the counselor's enthusiastic nods.

A fatter fly never lumbered on such a tight course toward a spider's web. I don't think Racinda knew that her pompous husband had been set up and was about to have some self-deceit exposed with one quick dart of light, hurled from the counselor's tongue.

"I do have a question," I said, at what seemed an appropriate break in this delightful, stimulating conversation. Plus, I could see on a wall clock that the only hour of counseling I would ever experience was about up. "Just how long do you have to listen to someone talking about their hurt and problems," I said, "before it's their responsibility to just *stop*?" I hadn't mentioned any names, but the meaning was clear: *Wasn't Racinda being a bit whiny about her issues? Wasn't it time for the girl to just buck up and move on?*

The spider bit hard, jaws crunching the fly's body parts. "That's a very sinful, selfish attitude, Bruce," the counselor said, straightening in her chair.

I was speechless, although the *How dare she say that?* response was already spreading inside me like a brushfire.

"Is love based on time and schedules?" she asked.

The session ended and we parted. At the seasoned age of forty-one, in the time it took to say a few sentences, I was naked. And I was mad.

After a day or two of nursing my humiliation into a full-blown anger, I presented my side of the case to Racinda, a prosecuting attorney with lava dripping from his lips. This tinkering with our relationship must be crushed. I shamed and accused her with exquisite viciousness, then after leaving her shredded and in tears, sulked off to lick my own wounds. But I found I could only think of hers. So back I crawled, as I'd done so often before, to ask forgiveness and win another pardon. This time my self-loathing was so complete I asked her, "Do you want to stay with me?"

I expected the usual response—she knew the line: "Why of course! I love you—we'll work this out." But instead she offered only a plaintive "I don't want to leave." I sensed at last the pain she felt.

The days passed and our marital ship righted to a sluggish course, but the deck rode nearer the waterline than before. As always, when perplexed I descended into my thought life, searching through cabinets for the file that would explain why our marriage had taken on water. I found no file but did arrive via holy prompting at an idea of the apostle Paul's. He had said of husbands that they should love their wives as Jesus loves the church—giving His life for her.

I thought about how Jesus had died, allowing His body to be spiked to a cross. Jesus didn't know if His beloved would respond in a pleasing way to such a noble gesture. There's no record that he stopped on the Via Dolorosa to try to work out a deal—"Look, I'll go through with this cross thing if you promise you will love Me back!"

No, He just stumbled up to His wooden execution chamber and surrendered His life.

I saw a parallel in our marriage: Someone needed to climb

on the cross, to make the first move toward saving a love. And that would need to be me, if I were to love my wife the way crusty Paul had suggested.

So I said some prayers and made some promises. But I wasn't any Jesus, willing to embrace my destiny so swiftly. It would be years before I could stand willingly and look up at a cross beam, a handful of nails in my pocket.

On a summer Sunday afternoon in 1987, the four of us were at our YMCA pool. Noelle and Allan loved the water, and as we laughed and splashed, we must have looked like the picture-perfect family. But beneath my jovial-daddy exterior, a tangled brew of anxiety, anger, and confusion bubbled.

I climbed out of the water and sat on the edge of the pool, my mind rummaging through the garbage dump of my emotional outlook. Racinda and one of the children slogged through the water to me, eager to tug me back to their reality, and splashed water on my chest and face. The shock of the cold water—a sudden and unwanted jerk on my attention chain—lit my rage.

I leaped in the water, grabbed Racinda by the shoulders, and pushed her under the surface. Once her head disappeared I let go, but when she emerged the happy family outing was over. She looked at me sadly, then without a word climbed from the pool, gathered her towel, and walked briskly to the dressing room.

Noelle and Allan, clutching their floats and water toys,

stood beside me stunned and silent. They did not know what I knew about their mother—how she desperately feared having her head dunked. My frightened children did not know that for an instant their father had hosted murder in his heart.

I felt as if I had taken a precious vase, the most beautiful and valuable thing I owned, and flung it against a rock, shattering the thin glass into a thousand colored pieces. I filled with shame. *What kind of a man treats the woman he loves like this?* With a sigh I said, "Daddy has lost his temper and hurt Mommy. We'll have to go now."

We dressed and drove home in a quiet car, my mate sitting silently in tears, her face and body turned from me.

I said I was sorry, and in a few days the scar tissue reformed on our wounds. Our busy, slowly dividing lives resumed. But a pocket of sickness was mutating in our relationship, gathering into a mass of malignant hurt.

About the time the counselor in Nashville was closing in for the kill on our marriage problems, we moved away. I found a new job in Colorado. With a host of challenges at hand—selling and buying homes, moving, resettling the children in new schools—Racinda and I were forced to take a break from exploring the caves in our hearts.

That was fine with me, but the pressures escalated. It wasn't some big thing, it was everything. We squabbled over details on the house we were building. She had a "do it right" attitude; I feared the cost. After delays and tensions related to financing, we finally moved into the new home. Racinda resumed her career as a public school music teacher, and our routine stabilized. But the stress of the past year had fertilized dormant weeds in my subconscious. I sank slowly into a dark, fear-filled pit.

At night I tossed and rolled, kept half awake by low-grade anxiety. The numbing effect of my busy daytime wore off, and I was forced to face the pains of life without anesthetic. Often I had anger and shook my fist at fates that had left me feeling so battered. Most nights any rest came only in snatches, and then dawn seeped through leaky window blinds, announcing another day of despairing fatigue.

My aching soul longed to weep. But instead of the relief of tears, the dull tension ate away my hope like battery acid. In the dark I talked to God, begging for a reprieve: "This is Your deal; just help me to fit in with Your plans!" I would plead. And sometimes holy warmth would quiet and settle, and I found rest. But too often I felt nothing. And then at daybreak I would arise weary, unsure I had strength to put on my facades, the shields we believe are necessary in a world full of other broken, angry facade bearers. And that was and is the point—the facades had to fall, and with heaven nearer than the womb, the supreme Mentor was running out of earth-time to rid me of childish armor.

Naked I'd come. Naked I'd be.

5

Night University

Spring 1988

JUST MONTHS AFTER SETTLING IN OUR NEW STATE, we drove
to northern California for the first of several surgeries on
Allan's ear. We had found a surgeon known worldwide for his
skill in fashioning a new outer ear without artificial implants
or prostheses.

Allan's surgery was set for a Monday morning. It tears you
deeply to watch your six-year-old child, his eyes widened with
fear, wheeled away to an operating room, his chubby arms
squeezing his favorite stuffed bear, both of them wearing hospital ID wristbands.

In the three-plus hours of surgery, the doctor removed a
chunk of cartilage from Allan's rib cage, and then, referring to
notes and measurements made earlier, carved the bone with a
scalpel into a shape that mirrored the form of Allan's "good
ear." Then the surgeon opened the skin on Allan's skull and
slid the sculpted bone into position. The cartilage, still much

alive, would find a fresh blood supply, adhere, and continue to live at its new body location. This was just the first step; three more surgeries would occur over the next two years.

Allan emerged from the recovery room with an enormous bandage covering most of his head—and the bear had one, too. The two surgery survivors rolled into Allan's room, where we waited.

"Allan has a new ear," the surgeon said.

Our little boy opened his eyes and moaned, then again fell asleep. Racinda paled, slumped in a chair, and cried.

After many hours of assembling Lego sets, playing video games, and chasing a boy intent on shedding a hot, itchy bandage, the initial recovery was a success and we drove home.

Nighttime turned against me. Instead of a refuge, the bed became a battleground. In the past my days had ended with a weary contentment as sleep snatched me to a cavern where thought is lost until 6:00 A.M. Now the night brought terrors—not nightmares, but fearful thoughts popping like corks to the surface of my mind.

I was unable to sleep more than a few hours but could not pinpoint why. My career was riding high. I lived in a fine house with a mountain range in view across a valley. Racinda and children were resettled from the move. Allan's ear continued to heal. My health was solid. Why was I so fearful? I was in new territory in life and had no map.

Before when troubled by a marital wound or career disappointment, I took a long walk, thought my way to resolution, consumed cookies and milk, read a good book, then went to bed—deep, cleansing, reviving rest. This old treatment had lost its healing power. I still could walk, ponder, snack, and read—but sleep long and hard? No way.

I fell in bed at night exhausted, but my mind spun, tormented by a blues tape running on continuous loop: *You are terribly tired! More than anything you need a good night's sleep; but you are not sleeping well, and tonight probably will be like so many of the others. You won't sleep. That means you will get up tomorrow more tired than you are now. And when you are tired, you just can't function very well. And if you don't perform well at work, you will fail. And with failure you will lose your job. And when you lose your job, you will be filled with shame and hurled onto the rubbish pile of humanity. What will become of you then, you weak, crumbling man—you loser? What will your wife and children think of you? What will your brothers think? What will the whole world say when the truth is finally revealed? Probably, "There goes a man that we thought we knew, but now we have the facts—he was a phony? We thought he was good and strong; turns out he's a weak impostor."*

I didn't know it, but sizable wings of my house were built on a foundation of sand. The higher tides of adult life were lapping at the door, threatening to sweep good old me away.

I went to our family doctor and said, "If I could just get some sleep, I'd be fine! Can you give me some pills?"

Since the man was a physician rather than just a pill pusher, before giving me a prescription, he looked beyond my body to my life and told me he thought I was mildly depressed.

Although I know better now, I would have preferred that he tell I had an inoperable tumor. *Depressed?* There wasn't a slot on my personal mental roster for an item named depression. Wasn't I made of stiffer stuff? Wasn't I the athlete, the Vietnam survivor, the joker making people laugh, the stone whom the weak people stood upon during their storms?

The good doctor, after hearing my answers to questions about my home life, also suggested I see a marriage counselor. Things were going from bad to worse.

I tried the pills, and almost against its will, my mind would wrench out of gear, falling unconscious for several hours. But the drug did not halt a spreading terror that I was losing my grip on life as I'd known it.

Racinda and I found a counselor, a man about my age named Brent, and we started seeing him together and separately. Once a week I would slink alone into the building that housed Brent's office, eyes down, my posture shouting the humiliation of a grown man who had to leave his work at midday for a mind massage. I liked Brent, though, a man whose rugged face was a comforting blend of pain and hope. He was perpetually hoarse, but the gravelly words soothed my trembling masculinity.

With his encouragement I told my story. I talked, he listened. Now and then he would clear his throat and croak an encouraging thought—"I hear you, Bruce; I feel the same way."

I began to feel better, although the nights remained torture. After more sessions I realized that Brent was the first person who had made me fully answer the question, "Well, how are you doing?" This pouring out of my questions and impressions about life embarrassed me—*Wasn't this boring barf of my feelings just another sign of pitiful weakness?* But Brent just sat and listened, sipping his coffee, occasionally laughing, sighing, clearing his throat, nodding.

I knew in a way I was paying someone to be my friend, my confessor, my soul ally. This was unsettling, but it felt so good. Wasn't this what a friend—or a wife—was supposed to do? But I hadn't allowed myself to have a friend or wife like this. So for now, my gruff buddy would have to do—at $60 an hour.

Talking to Brent, alone and when Racinda joined us, opened up new ways of speaking and listening. My discovery that I had internal injuries oozing blood added new words to my vocabulary, phrases from a language called pain.

Since Brent thought a special weekend seminar might help Racinda and me deal with some particular issues, we flew to Tucson. The seminar's content gripped us, and away from work duties and children, we had more time to mop up toxins in the environment of our relationship.

I saw now how I had abused her, not with clenched fist but

with clenched tongue. Some of my words were hateful, but many more were the clever and elegant tools of control. She had baited my anger for reasons of her own, but I was a vicious competitor in this relational battle and used words, words, words to remind her of my "superiority."

We returned to the hotel at evening after long workouts of self-discovery. I understood how my tongue had knifed her tender heart. I sat on the bed, shoulders heavy in regret. And then my friend came and held me, undressed me, took me into her arms, and sweetly loved me. And we both knew again that the Matchmaker hadn't made a mistake, even though there was finishing work to be done on His creation called us.

In 1991—not for the first time, but more intensely—Brent asked me to probe my relationship with God. As with too many of His adopted children, my interactions with "Big Dad" were wary and strained.

My mind overflowed with facts and sentiments about the Father—I could defend His virtues with the best of them. But God stirred little passion in my cold heart. I lived in my house, and He lived elsewhere in His house. We exchanged pleasantries through my prayers, and I faithfully sent Him my checks and helped out when I could with His favorite activities. But we were not close. Big Dad and I didn't go fishing or meet for coffee so that we could catch up on what each other was doing.

It had not always been so, certainly not when we first met.

None of us has a clue when the Master will come calling. By age eight I already knew a lot about faith. My parents were devout in church attendance and private piety. Our community church opened its doors three times a week. We hardly ever missed, and from my earliest years even my tiny life revolved around church events. In Sunday school I heard all of the great Bible stories and certainly knew the key points about why Jesus had visited earth. But a piece in my religious experience was missing.

One spring I rode with my parents to Three Hills, Alberta, Canada, where an older brother was to graduate from Bible college. During the days preceding the graduation ceremony, meetings were held at the school. One morning I attended a children's session where the teacher asked if anyone wanted to invite Jesus into his or her heart. My discomfort was intense. At age eight, why would a child have much reason to resist heaven's woo? But already there was a battlefield in my soul because I struggled . . . and chose not to raise my arm and sign on with the redeemed. And I spent a miserable day, regretting my choice against what I knew was right and lovely.

At that evening's meeting a man who once did illegal wiretaps and other electronic crimes for the mob told of giving his heart to Jesus at a Billy Graham crusade. By now, after many hours of regret for resisting the holy call, my soul longed for a second chance. And it came when the ex-criminal issued an invitation.

I looked at my mom and pointed toward the front of the auditorium, so the two of us went together. A man met with us in a backstage room and explained what was required. No holding back this time. With tears streaming I spoke the prayer and accepted the supreme offer. Maybe I had come chased more by fear than drawn by love. But how I made it to eternity's door wasn't as important as having safely arrived.

Across the years, however, weeds had sprung up in my faith garden. I had some bad ideas about God, and the spiritual chip on my shoulder was a barrier He would not cross— that was my choice; I didn't want such a close relationship.

My father on earth—Little Dad—had been distant, quiet, intellectual, and largely unaffectionate. When he showed feeling, often his "go-to" emotion was anger. He was a solid, good man and a faithful father. I *knew* he loved me, I just couldn't *feel* his love. So it wasn't a surprise to learn that, when stripped of all my religiously correct feelings about God, what remained was a pathetic collection of fear, grudging awe, suspicion, and anger.

My counselor watched me slowly embrace my spiritual poverty and leave behind my penthouse on Pride Street. Now that I was a homeless soul desperate for crumbs and a drink, Brent told me to stop by God's door for a handout—to initiate conversation, to know this Daddy in a new way.

In September 1991 it happened. I went looking for Him, but He found me first. The doorbell rang, and I asked Daddy in. I was alone in my home office. No voice from the ceiling light or burning bookcase, just a palpable sense of the great spiritual One coming near. I wept the tears of relief, release, wonder. Then He reminded me of the parable of the prodigal son. And Daddy revealed startling news: *I was a prodigal son, a son who had wandered far and ended up running with pigs. After all, the prodigal always was a son, a member of the family. And, yes, Daddy had been waiting for me to come home, His eyes moist with love, smiling, arms spread wide.* So I buried myself in His embrace. And we caught up on things.

My struggles continued, but now I knew God's street address, and I knew the porch light would be on, the door unlocked. During the night when I would awaken, instead of always lurching to visit my fears, I would lead my troubled spirit through prayer to God. And I now felt comfortable enough to invite Big Dad to visit my place. I would open my heart's door and ask the whole group in—Father, Son, and Holy Ghost. We would visit, and even if I could not return to sleep, my soul found peace and hope and confidence that even in tomorrow's fatigue I would not walk alone in my weakness.

Sometimes in these evening get-togethers, when I drifted in that fog between the shores of sleep and awake, I would imagine that my three Buddies and I were driving through the barren outback of Wyoming. Most of the time Jesus drove, and I sat in the front seat with Him. The other two were in back. We would chat in a relaxed way; there was no stress or anxiety among us. I mean, what was there to be uptight about driving along an empty two-lane highway, the stars gleaming and thick, headed for somewhere in the wilds of Wyoming? In a while the conversation would diminish, and each of us would tend peacefully to private thoughts, eyes feasting on the twinkling canopy, a glut of diamonds resting on the velvet of night. The warm car rolled on across the still desert, the road stretching straight for miles, tires and pavement meeting in a satisfying whine.

And sleep came.

In November I announced to Brent that I felt ready to walk life's path by myself. I thanked him, we shook hands, and with a mix of fear and hope surging through my chest, I left his counseling den for good.

Racinda and I still fought, although now with deeper insight into why.

In my case I had underground storage tanks of anger that required regular flushing. Stockpiling anger is not virtuous, like saving money or stacking firewood for winter. Anger kept in the emotions is as sour food in the stomach; in time you just have to vomit. One of my best excuses for heaving the bile was my perception that some "foolishness" on Racinda's part was just more than a good, nice man like me should have to take.

Many of the tongue trashings began on Saturday morning, a promising setting for emotional mayhem, because Saturday was the one day of the week when expectations soared higher than the space shuttle. Both of us were home from work and finally had some time to catch up on put-off tasks. Many times we worked together well and the day was hitchless. But too often the possibility of personal free time for hobbies or interests turned us into adversaries scrapping for the same desirous piece of turf.

On one Saturday that quickly went south, Racinda wanted to talk at length about a conflict at work. I listened patiently a few minutes, maintaining eye contact and even throwing in a compassionate "hmmm" now and then. But as the sun rose higher in the sky, I started to lose it—glancing at my watch, shifting my body, furrowing my brow. My well-planned morning was disappearing, and I grew frustrated, which translated means "angry."

Instead of just saying, "Honey, I really need to get on with my to-do list; could we talk more about this later?"—a mature way to behave—I started pacing the room. Then to better demonstrate my disgust—*she just wasn't getting it!*—I threw some of my clothes on the floor and slammed a door.

I concluded my tantrum with a charming monologue: "Well, I just never have time around here to do what I need to do. Why do we have to talk and talk like this?"

Racinda's patience gave out, and she released some of her own steam. "Why don't you just go do whatever you want, you jerk. I've got my own work to do." With that *she* shut the door with gusto.

At that I turned and left the house—*I wasn't going to let*

HER treat ME like that! I stalked off down the streets of the neighborhood, filled with self-righteous pity and rage, adrenaline surging at narcotic levels in my bloodstream. Getting rid of anger feels great, but it's a high that drops you fast.

In fifteen minutes I felt the first withdrawal pangs and began losing my concentration, distracted by thoughts like, *Why are you out here roaming when you have so much to do today?*

I started for home and said my first prayer of the morning, through gritted teeth: "God, all I want is a happy family. Please help me not to screw this up." By the time I entered the back door, I had raised a white flag.

"I was such a poophead," I said to Racinda. "I'm sorry for acting the way I did."

"Yes, you were, but I kind of egged you on once you got going," Racinda said. "I wish you would just say what is bothering you instead of dumping all over me."

"Yeah, I know. Will you forgive me?"

"Yes."

I put my arms around her and endured one of those *I'll let you do this, but I don't have to enjoy it yet* limp body hugs.

We were learning how to fight "better," having developed a fondness for the rewards of peacetime. The whole screaming, slamming, sweating, sighing, swearing, sobbing fight scene seemed silly.

With the truce in place, the children slowly emerged from their bomb shelters, pleased to see that Dad and Mom were once again acting like adults but wondering how long it might take to restore a pleasant family mood this time.

❧

That night we lay in each other's arms, drained by the morning's tussle but now at peace, our bodies linked in a symphony of love. Two tired people, happier, wiser—more aware of love's many chords than those impatient, angry lovers of years past.

Quiet, gentle, patient waves of love washed between us in this bed of tenderness. A precious splendor this—to be loved by someone, one who knows your sin-wracked ugliness.

Sex is wonderful and horrible. The wonderful is the mind-blowing creativity of it. What kind of Designer could devise an appetite so consuming, and such a means to sate it?

But sex is horrible, too. What can showcase better our selfishness and crippled capacity to love? We brush against intimacy. In passion we taste beyond puny appetites, yet never fill. So close, but still alone. For pilgrims an earthly ecstasy won't satisfy a heavenly hunger.

But sex is good. On a cloud of stuffing and springs I've floated in this woman's embrace. In the other's arms we build bridges, suspended wobbly, but bridges still on which child-like selves cross and find welcome. In love we have added more humanity to the human race.

And when it's good, when the legs, arms, chests, lips, cheeks, and hearts are close, when it's good like that, it's good like nothing else. And I thank the Designer for the good He's given me.

On that night in May, sleep took me under to healing depths. Gray, hard life might wait at dawn, but I would rise with a sacred memory. I'd sipped the wine of eternity.

Joy arrives in surprise, slipping through the heart's door without a knock.

Almost too old for this kind of thing now, sometimes on a weekend morning Noelle and Allan came with noses and feet cold into our bed. There we were, four peas in a full pod, reeking of night smells, hair askew, sleep-gummed eyes—one sodden breathing lump. No words, grunts and giggles, lazy inhaling of morning air. All the ecstasy and hope of existence cuddled under colored sheets.

This was sweet, and hilarious, and makes me want to cry. Joy and grief are Siamese twins. These times should not end, but will. We always want such refuge for our children, but only moments can make.

After a cruel illness slowly sucked away his ability to participate in day-to-day reality, Racinda's father died without warning, slipping away between dusk and dawn on a cool March night.

We four made our way to the family farmhouse in Iowa to

join Racinda's mother and others with tired, reddened eyes. A day or two passed with viewings and weary discussions with those in the mortician trade.

The funeral happened in the afternoon. We rode to the church behind the hearse and the black Cadillac provided for the widow. The small building was full of mostly older people sitting in a hush interrupted only by coughs. Although the body rested in view behind the last pew, in a bronze box, I had no desire to gaze again at the bleak face. Dead bodies are such a farce. They masquerade as homes for living spirits, but no matter how clever the undertaker's craft, no one is fooled. There's nobody home there anymore.

Mercifully, we family mourners sat on the last two rows where we could lose our tears away from prying eyes. A woman pastor led the service. The Scriptures of comfort were read. The congregation sang "Amazing Grace." From the back pews came a faint cry.

The service ended and the casket, closed now for good, exited with the muscles of suited men. We drove slowly under a bright sun, a sober caravan to the nearby field dotted with stones. On the way Racinda dabbed her eyes and emitted a sob, a final eloquent summary of promises fallen. Allan, in voice tender and filled with care, asked: "Are you okay, Mom?"

"Yes, I'm okay."

Fresh earth was piled next to the hole, near a tent erected to break the wind. "Ashes to ashes, dust to dust." Prayers. The mourners filed by a last time. Soft words, embraces, tears.

Wind fluttered the tent walls. The light went flat as the sun fell. Everyone had gone except the next of kin. We finally walked away. The car doors slammed shut, and workers with cigarettes and shovels emerged from behind a shed.

We rode relieved yet wordlessly back to the church basement where the ladies from the farms were serving coffee, juice, brownies, and coconut lemon bars. The silence was gone, banished by talk of weather, crops, and many other things.

6

The Other Lover

Spring 1995

AMONG THE BILLIONS OF CELLS dividing on cue at the proper rate in the human body, one cell decides, "I'll do it my way," and creates a new order, mutating into a hostile force. This cell is purposeless, has no assignment to work for the good in the body's society. This cell is selfish, its only occupation to rummage for food and sustain itself at the expense of others.

The parasite has a notable characteristic—a striking ability to deceive, to cloak its malevolent intentions with such cleverness that agents of the immune system do not see the homeless rogue and pass as though blinded by light.

In time, like all cells, the mutant becomes two mutants, then four, then eight, and so on. In more time the mutants form a club, then a colony, but remain too small to be detected, for example, during a breast exam by a woman or her doctor.

In order to widen its borders, the deviant community develops through further mutation an expansion plan and begins annexing surrounding territory to increase the food supply. The cell city's next requirement is a stable infrastructure, so vessel lines are advanced to ensure a constant blood supply. With such limitless resources, the pace of sprawl increases, the insurrection exploding into an evil empire large enough to be named on the body's map: *tumor*.

Although almost allergic to medical doctors, Racinda still went faithfully for her exams, pap smears, and, as she entered her forties, the occasional mammogram. Those reports were benign. But her rapid heartbeat problem had not gone away.

When Racinda had a spell, I dug through my wallet for the card on which I'd scribbled instructions from the doctor on what she should do. I coached her to lie on her side or to sit down, bend over, and tighten muscles in her stomach and back. Mainly though, I prayed as I sat beside her, helpless, watching her chest heave, wondering how long I should wait before dialing 911. No matter if the doctor said not to worry, this was terrifying.

The incidents increased and were worse. Her heart pounded wildly—more than 200 beats per minute—sometimes for an hour or longer. When the arrhythmia subsided, she was spent, her chest aching. During one long incident, we decided to go to the emergency room, but halfway there the heart rate dropped, so we went home.

We went to a cardiologist, and after some tests, the diagnosis was Wolff-Parkinson-White syndrome, a malfunction in the heart's electrical system. The condition probably was not life-threatening, but the incidents would increase in length and intensity. Treatment was available—either medication or a surgical procedure called ablation. Racinda tried the pills first, but the side effects were unpleasant. She decided to risk the surgery with hope of ridding herself of a problem she'd come to hate.

Through friends we located a surgeon in Oklahoma City who was widely known for his success with the ablation procedure. In June of 1995 the entire family drove to Oklahoma.

The night before the operation, the doctors explained the procedure, which would involve inserting tiny catheters in veins in her thighs and threading them up to the heart region. During the procedure the "eyes" for the doctors would be provided via a constant X ray, made possible, of course, by radiation.

As physicians always must do, the risks were reviewed. If the problem existed in the wrong region of the heart, the procedure would be too dangerous and the doctors would abort. Racinda would have to live with rapid heartbeat spells or go back on medication. If the procedure went awry, leaving the "electrical system" damaged, a pacemaker would be installed. And there was a small chance that the unexpected would occur and she would not survive the operation.

The next morning the kids and I gathered early in Racinda's room to wait. Minutes before she was to leave for the operating room, someone knocked on the door. I peeked out and my eyes widened—standing before me were two couples, our pastor and wife and other friends who had driven 600 miles from Colorado to be with us. We surrounded her bed, joined hands, and prayed.

Moments later they wheeled Racinda away. The waiting began. We sat for hours, then shortly after noon it was over. The operation was a success. Racinda should never have another rapid heartbeat incident.

The following day after lunch, Racinda was released from the hospital and we began our drive home, routing ourselves through Kansas. We arrived at our hotel mid-evening, and after settling in, the sky went storm black. A severe weather warning scrolled across the TV screen. The phone rang. The desk clerk announced an approaching tornado and asked us to seek shelter on a lower level. We dressed and helped Racinda walk gingerly down some stairs and into a cavernous room where other guests milled. Thunder boomed, and the dark sky cracked open with lightning. Heavy rain fell and the wind blew as storm sirens howled. But the tornado went elsewhere. The all-clear notice came and we returned to our room.

Like the disappearing tornado, I thought we had faced what certainly must be the last serious health threat for years in our family. Allan's ear surgeries were in the past, and now Racinda's heart was fixed. Had we not paid our dues? Could I not look forward to normal life? I fell then into a light sleep, unsettled still by the memory of the mournful wail of a storm siren.

Summer of 1995 arrived—time for a family reunion with my brothers and their families in Montana near Glacier Park. My work had consumed energy and time for months, and even as we loaded the car I was busy finishing business.

As we drove through Denver, I made the last calls on the cell phone, then slumped in the seat. The sky was clear, and as we rolled north beyond Cheyenne, Wyoming, the sight of the uncluttered plains drained my stress. We faced two full days of driving, and even then would arrive at the reunion after the others. With my workload this was the best I could do.

By mid-afternoon I had the vacation mood—mind out of gear, teasing Racinda, tickling the kids, musing on the next food stop. As the car gobbled up the miles, music poured from the cassette player. This was good.

Near sunset we stopped for burgers, then rolled into Billings to spend the night with good friends. After solid rest and breakfast, we left early to finish the drive. And drive we did—crossing Montana brings on the butt blisters, but the scenery improves hour by hour as you move west. By mid-afternoon we realized there was no way we would arrive at Peaceful Lodge for dinner. We stopped so we could call and cancel our reservation.

A woman answered. I explained that I was with the Nygren party, and regrettably, our family of four would not make the evening meal. She seemed bewildered by this news, but thanked me for calling.

We stopped for fast food and then drove on. At 7:00 P.M. we

reached Fortine, just twenty miles from our destination. I found a pay phone and called Peaceful Lodge for precise directions. Again a perplexed person on the other gave vague instructions that did not inspire confidence. Something just wasn't right, but I muzzled my anxiety and climbed behind the wheel.

We drove on. All of us were very tired, having sat in what seemed a shrinking car for more than twenty hours and a thousand-plus miles. The good feelings of a journey almost completed washed over me, and I mused aloud about the strange phone calls. Trying to humor the weary spirits in the car, I said, "Wouldn't it be just crazy if this isn't the right weekend for the reunion?"

I chuckled but kept eyes on the thick pines along the roadside, checking for deer on the move at twilight. Some paper rustled in the backseat where our teenagers sat, and glancing in the mirror I saw Allan jab his finger wildly at the letter about the reunion. Noelle looked on, her eyes big from shock.

My heart sank. I didn't need to ask, but I did: "Are we here on the wrong weekend?" The kids nodded, averting their eyes, no doubt certain this was a case where the messenger of bad news would face swift execution.

My body shook. I slowed the car and pulled to the side of the road. In a hoarse whisper I asked for the letter, and there it was in my handwriting. I had informed the reunion organizer that we would arrive on July 21—next to the printed dates for the reunion at Peaceful Lodge on July 27 to 31.

I turned off the engine. We sat quietly, my shoulders

slumped, the cursed paper—evidence of my incredible mistake—limp in my lap. No one spoke. The world was silent. I moaned and shook my head repeatedly, as though trying to wake from a nightmare.

"This will be okay," Racinda said, scrambling like a fireman to pour foam on a gas spill before it explodes. "We can make this work."

Finally, I started the engine and wheeled the car back to the south. There was no reason to go to Peaceful Lodge nearly a week before everyone else.

"This isn't the end of the world," Racinda said, calling on all of her experience in anger control from other moments like this in our marriage.

"I just can't believe it," I said. I looked at Racinda, who gave me a hopeful look. I wanted to blame her—anyone—for the *faux pas*, but there was too much damning evidence and too many witnesses. I had screwed up. It was my fault.

We drove for miles in a cathedral-like hush. I stopped shaking my head. Finally I forced out a tiny laugh. And then the others could breathe again. Dad had not combusted, his head separating from his shoulders and leaving through the roof of the car.

But I wondered how a little brother would explain this to his older siblings, who were always on the lookout for another family joke.

A year after this family reunion, alone in a hotel room while on a business trip, I finally sealed the peace with my father many years after his death.

In the early 1980s, when I was busy establishing a family of my own, my dad came several times to live with us for a few months. After my mother's death in 1979, Dad changed. But I was still too young, too distracted, too angry with him to notice. The emotions that flow in a family are an underground river. That's why I was fifty years old before I found the will and words to bless my father.

I was born sinful but learned the finer points of storing and dumping anger from Dad. We did get along. We agreed on faith and politics. We both loved reading and spent many evenings fishing on the lake, near enough to smell each other's sweat, peering intently at our bobbers. But there were too many thoughts and feelings—good and bad—unspoken. Beneath our placid connection were memories hurtful and unresolved.

An old man, Dad came to Nashville and stayed in our extra bedroom. He was a carpenter, so as he had strength, he would putter on projects. Mainly he sat, dozing off, the news-paper falling as a blanket on his chest. He read story after story to Noelle, until at times they both napped together in the chair. And he sipped hot drinks and talked with Racinda. In a touching way that even I noticed, she and Dad fulfilled something missing in both of them.

The live-in carpenter and I undertook a small remodeling of our basement. I would help at night and on weekends, but

Dad was the main man. One evening we were working as a team when I discovered a flaw in the taping of a wallboard seam. It wasn't that big a deal, and with failing eyesight, his mistake was innocent. But I was looking for an opportunity to send a message without saying much—a tactic I had learned from him. I sighed in disgust, glared at the wall, flung a tool on the floor. And Dad got the message. He let out a tiny sob, wiped a tear or two away with his large, worn fingers, and without a word climbed the stairs with weary feet.

And I wanted to cry out something from the bottom of my soul but didn't know what to say. I was still the angry little boy who had spilled the oil from the barrel—finding ways to make the big man pay.

Perhaps I did apologize; I can't remember. We had more good times and pleasant days. Dad's heart wore out, and a week after his last Nashville visit, he died in Minnesota. The family gathered again in the pines and said good-bye.

God is no captive of our time and the Spirit operates in ways mysterious. So I can't say it was odd that in a hotel room in St. Louis fifteen years later I could not sleep until I said out loud into the chasm of the unseen: "Dad, I want to tell you that I love you and forgive you. And I am sorry for all the things I did to hurt you."

Doesn't every marriage face the temptation of other lovers? I do not mean adultery, but liaisons with other lusts?

One of the other lovers in our marriage often appeared in December. In the 1996 holiday season, in addition to the programs required at the school where Racinda taught elementary music, our church asked her to plan a special Christmas service.

Racinda took to the challenge at full throttle. For me this was a good news/bad news scenario: The good part was the splash-over excitement and fun for the entire family when another "production" was in the works. The downside was a long history of conflict between us over Racinda's near total preoccupation with such events. Many years the season of glad tidings and great joy was anything but that.

This time the rehearsals, the last-minute panic before performance, the mixture of fatigue and exhilaration that goes with making music brought steady joy. The worshipers received the music gladly, and at the end of that busy December Sunday, Racinda and I savored the delicious memory—a celebration where everyone in our family together had contributed Advent praise with voice or instrument.

And we'd not had a single argument. With another week before December 25 to write cards and finish shopping, was this shaping up as the best Christmas ever?

Then the other lover appeared.

With applause still ringing from her program's success, Racinda was invited to assemble the music experience for the Christmas Eve communion. And with enthusiasm, she said yes, and although I said my blessing, inside I was mumbling *No! No! No!* in jealousy of Racinda's other lover, this consuming passion for music that drew her away from me, leaving me feeling discarded, unneeded, used, alone. My reactions weren't rational—How could her call to make glorious music for God be wrong?—but no one has ever accused the hotter passions of having brains.

I behaved like any garden-variety jilted lover, burying my perceived mistreatment in a hole deep inside, where it rotted at an alarming rate and seeped into vents in the far corners of mind and emotion. I soon was full of angry poison, eager for revenge.

Early on Christmas Eve I awoke with a rage fever. In the dark Racinda slept quietly, but I stared wide-eyed at the ceiling, nerves tight. Every half hour I would rise and move noisily to the bathroom or elsewhere. As I paced, I rehearsed the charges I would deliver to this woman who now seemed the enemy. When sunlight first brightened the master bedroom, I let her have it, my wrath breaking like pus. Stunned and bruised, Racinda retreated, then lashed back.

After a gangrene of words lasting hours, we took the medicine of humility to save the year's happiest day for our family. But I knew the damage was done, my anger had ravished as a plague, bringing the sting of death to new intentions and ways of relating. Hadn't we both changed, understanding better how to communicate our way through such emotional flu?

Yes, but this struggle is not just against our tainted flesh. Is it a coincidence, on the very day our hearts reach an annual loud chorus of praise to the God of triumph, that we should yield to the temptation to replay some cracked record from our past?

Yet on this Advent's eve, grace was greater than our garbage. We sang a carol of forgiveness, cleansed our anger, and pressed on to the manger. And when the elements arrived, the body and blood may have stuck for an instant in my grieving throat, but the bread and wine surely went down.

Nothing, not flawed lovers, not our lingering depravity, not the powers of hell—nothing stops that Boy born in Bethlehem.

The family forecast as 1997 dawned was "partly sunny."

The college search for Noelle was over; she had won acceptance at her first-pick college. Allan was jamming on guitar with friends and playing basketball for a club team. I was happy in a new job as a writer, finally living a lifelong dream.

But Racinda struggled. Some combination of hormonal change, emotional pain, frustrations in career, and disappointments with me kept her in low-hanging clouds. That last issue was the worst. She told me long thereafter that her outlook on our marriage was so dark that she wanted to die; in her black mood, death seemed the only reasonable escape.

That was the backdrop for the ugly March weekend, to the night of the lump, to the days we now call B.C.—before cancer.

7

*

The Sentence

March 1997

THE TENDENCY IS TO FORGET that a woman's breast, which in our culture provokes obsessive attention and thrills the male imagination, is by elegant but simple design a milk production facility. Little girls and boys both have similar rudimentary breast tissue until puberty, when the estrogen and progesterone hormones flood the young woman's body and change the prairie plains on her chest into foothills, then the glorious peaks of womanhood.

It's an evil plot that throughout much of recorded history the disease most feared by women breeds its embryos of death inside the serene, lovely colony of flesh where a nursing mother produces the liquid of life for the newborn child.

In the fully developed breast, the tissue is divided into a dozen or more compartments called lobes. Within the lobes are smaller sacs lined with cells capable of producing milk. The milk leaves the sacs through tiny tubes, which like tributaries of a river, merge into main channels or ducts that deliver the fluid to the nipple.

The mammary glands of the adult female are prone to developing lumps, most of them benign. But just what were those two swollen clumps (another, smaller one was detected) Racinda found nestled in her breast that fateful Sunday night?

Our official inquiry concerning the lumps began in our family doctor's office the afternoon after their discovery. It's too bad Superman didn't enter the medical profession, because his X-ray vision would enhance lump evaluation. Mere mortal physicians must feel the swollen masses with their fingertips, mumbling thoughtful "hmmms" and offering guarded profundities like, "Yes. It's definitely a lump."

The doctor gamely tried to disarm our anxiety but could not predict whether the lumps were ominous or not. He ordered an ultrasound, which because of Racinda's teaching routine could not be scheduled until three days later. Circumstances had enrolled us in a required course for dealing with threatening disease—Waiting 101.

That night Racinda and I said our prayers, and the next morning she went to work while I headed to the mountains for a long-awaited day of skiing with a friend. As he and I drove into the Rockies, I stowed my fears. There was no history of breast disease in Racinda's family. No one had told me yet that in just one of twenty breast cancer cases is there evidence of the disease in the woman's family tree.

The day passed with one ski lift conversation after another about many topics, but no mention of the drama in Racinda's chest. Finally, on the ride home, our conversation turned personal and we spoke briefly of our spouses. Only then did I dribble out my unsettling news. I saw no need just yet to leave my residency in the state of denial.

After the ultrasound on Thursday afternoon, we asked to speak with the radiologist. He met us in a darkened room with walls lined with backlit viewing screens. After some conversational foreplay, he showed us the film, pointing out the blots on the image. His lump-detector machine could not tell what the masses were, but he did say bluntly, "I would have this looked at right away."

"Who should we see?" I asked.

"A surgeon, who might want to do a biopsy."

We stumbled to the car and said little as we rode home. A rivulet of panic was trickling through my dam of denial, but I chose not to share any foreboding with Racinda. That night we talked and agreed that we must get answers as quickly as possible. We had no surgeon in waiting, so we decided to see our family doctor for advice the next morning.

After fitful sleep, we rose at dawn and went early to the doctor's office, the first patients through the clinic door. We explained our dilemma to the receptionist and learned our doctor would not be in. We saw another doctor, and he and a caring nurse scheduled an immediate appointment with a "great surgeon—you'll like her."

We hustled to collect all old mammogram films and the ultrasound report and dashed to the surgeon's office. I was struggling to define my role as the doctor visits mounted. At first I didn't even know if I should stay in the examining room as repeatedly Racinda stripped to the waist, slipped on a paper gown, and then sat with expectant expression while each physician boldly explored territory that had been so long my preserve.

The surgeon entered the room, a young woman of exuberant spirit. She looked at the films and did her own probing. "I don't believe this is much to worry about," she said. "I think you have some cysts. If it's okay with you, I want to insert a needle into the larger lump. I think I'll be able to withdraw some clear fluid." This seemed a great idea to us; finally a definitive answer and the possibility of some good news.

The doctor left the room to collect supplies, and when the door shut I jabbed my thumb in the air. *I just knew it! This was all going to turn out to be nothing.*

The surgeon returned, numbed Racinda's skin, then slid the needle into the lump. She maneuvered the tip while pulling on the syringe plunger. Not much happened. No stream of liquid; just drops of blood. "Hmm," the doctor said, "not what I expected."

She gave two choices—wait for a month to see whether the lumps grew, or proceed immediately with a biopsy.

"I want the biopsy," Racinda said quickly and firmly. "How soon can we do it?"

✑

The procedure was set for Monday, and now we advanced to Waiting 201—trying to live normally over a weekend while that long list of "what-ifs" circulates constantly through your mind. You go shopping, you go to a movie, you go to church. And you meet people you know, some of them friends, and you have to decide, *Do I just play happy face with everybody, or do I blurt it out? "Racinda's got some lumps in her breast! She's having a biopsy Monday. Oh, what does our future hold?"*

Early Monday morning we entered the hospital, and the pre-op liturgy of checking, probing, and needle sticking began. The anesthesiologist stopped by, as did the surgeon.

Before nurses wheeled Racinda away, we prayed, expressing our willingness to accept the results. But we asked for a "good outcome," which to us meant the lumps would be run-of-the-mill, benign throwaways. After a parting kiss I watched Racinda's entourage roll down the shimmering hallway and disappear through electric doors that hissed open and swallowed them all.

In the waiting room I drank coffee, passing time with other waiters who stared with disinterest at newspapers and a TV screen. In about forty-five minutes the surgeon appeared in green surgical garb, a mask dangling from her neck. "Everything went fine," she said. "She's in recovery; she'll be back here where you can see her in a few minutes."

And then came the break in conversation, not more than a second or two, when time freezes. The doctor drew a breath, and I wanted to scream, "Well, tell me now! Is she okay? What did you see? What did those lumps look like?" But I didn't say that. I was content for a few more moments to cling to a reality of my manufacture.

"The biopsy went fine," the surgeon said. "She did great. There were two lumps, and it looked like they were somewhat connected. I took them out and now we'll have to wait for the pathology report—probably tomorrow. I'll call you."

We confirmed my phone number, and then as she left, she smiled and said, "Keep thinking happy thoughts. Don't worry."

Racinda was released within the hour and we returned home. She rested and I went back to work. But my mind drifted, wondering where her lumps might be. Were they still bound for the pathology lab across town, rattling along in the dusty interior of a delivery van? Or had they already arrived and now waited anonymously with dozens of other tissue specimens in a doctor's in basket? Or even now was some impersonal evaluator of Racinda's fate discovering demon cells in the illuminated lens of the microscope? And what emotions would such a person have dictating results that would trigger elation or dread?

The hours of tangled thought and pleading prayer dragged along, all assignments to complete in this course of life called Waiting.

That March afternoon I went for a previously scheduled haircut. This seemed a safe foray from the telephone, where Racinda—home recuperating from the biopsy—waited for the doctor's call.

Since I'd never welcomed attention on my personal life, I joined in the hair shop pitter-patter with my favorite stylist but kept my private drama secret as shears hummed and scissors snipped. What would be the point of discussing "possible bad news"? But keeping secrets, even from a casual acquaintance, does leave you feeling a bit grimy.

I drove home and pulled the car in the garage. Before going back to work in my basement office, I decided to check on Racinda. Outside her door I heard her voice; she was on the phone. And I knew by the fear and urgency in her voice that the doctor was on the line. The news was not good.

For an instant I froze, pausing, wondering if by waiting I might avoid this fate. I entered the room, my heart already empty, and saw her in the chair, trying unsuccessfully to look brave, her color bleached, eyes afloat in tears.

Seeing me, she said with voice wobbling, "It's cancer, honey."

At that moment, about 2:45 on a spring afternoon, life as we'd known it ended.

The *C* word. The one word I'd never wanted in my family's vocabulary. When I got on the line to hear the doctor's sober summary, I began my orientation to the foul words that trail behind the *C* word, like ugly ducklings in the wake of a mud hen: malignant, oncologist, mastectomy, prosthesis, chemotherapy, metastasis, survival rate, carcinoma, DCIS (ductal carcinoma in situ), estrogen receptors, invasive, lymph nodes, staging, tumor, and more.

After answering the questions we could think of, the doctor promised to see us the next day and said good-bye.

I hugged Racinda, then struggled for words. But what can you say other than "I can't believe it!" and "I'm sorry"? I was stunned and sat down, my thoughts swirling. I did comfort her, but my mind sprinted to find hope for me, too.

A crisis doesn't allow much time for reflection. The children arrived home from school, and since as a family we had no history of sticking happy faces on bad news, we had to tell them. But this gave new meaning to "bad."

We assembled, the negative vibes as thick as smog, in the family room—normally the place to watch a movie, read a book, chat, horse around, eat popcorn. Once in a great while the room was the site of a family meeting on some thorny issue, but never a summit like this. Racinda and I explained the sobering information, spinning out as many "positives" as we could—"They caught this early," and "Breast cancer can be beaten"—with muted enthusiasm. There's just no good way to make a plate of horse manure look like powdered donuts!

Tears streamed on Noelle's cheeks, and Allan sat motionless, his expression limp. This was a moment of searing sadness. It can't get much worse—the feeling of powerlessness as you introduce your children to life's pain.

I prayed aloud, asking God to heal, guide, and comfort. We did some family hugging, and then Racinda and I retreated to discuss pressing issues—leaving the children temporarily to start a journey of their own through new territory of thoughts and feelings.

I knew little about cancer. The disease had never afflicted my immediate family, and cancer is not a topic studied for the joy of knowledge. Scattered pieces of information floated from my memory, one the idea that much progress had occurred in "curing" breast cancer.

A friend had loaned us *Dr. Susan Love's Breast Book* (Addison Wesley, 1995). Now I hungrily read the Love book for information. Gathering facts was comforting and helped me believe that life was still under our control.

Without knowing, I had shifted into my battlefield commander role. We were in a firefight—mortar rounds dropping in our compound and the sappers crawling through the concertina wire on the perimeter. There was no time for feelings. We had to assess damage, protect the wounded, and map out strategy for the counterattack. While Racinda called close friends and edged with small steps toward facing her emotions, I stuffed them in a sack. Now was the time to fight and survive.

In the hours and days that followed, I discovered that studying cancer is like losing your way in a cave of a thousand passageways. If you're not careful, you can crawl a long way into a promising cavern before hitting a dead end.

There are well over one hundred types of cancer, and about one of three persons alive today will fight the disease sometime during their lifetime. Evidence of cancer is found in dinosaur bones and Egyptian mummies. Some cancers are confronted well by established medical treatments. But the disease defies predictability, and there are no known cures that always work on every patient.

Racinda and I saw the surgeon the day after receiving the biopsy report. The surgeon explained treatment options but made clear that an oncologist must lead in the long-term fight. Although the initial tumor lumps were gone, the surgeon said that much additional tissue in Racinda's breast looked suspicious. She could go back in and carve away, but the doctor wondered just how clean the margins would be. This was another concept related to the *C* word. Each time a surgeon cuts suspicious flesh, samples of tissue on the edge, or margins, of the incision go to the pathologist for analysis. If no cancerous cells are found, the margins are said to be clean. This is good.

The doctor was preparing Racinda for a possible mastectomy. During that surgery the surgeon would remove a sample of tissue from the armpit, an attempt to collect a good number of lymph nodes. These nodes would be examined for cancer to help determine if any breast cancer cells might have migrated from the tumors to other body organs. This is bad.

We were advancing into a delicate, disheartening zone unique to breast cancer. Understandably, women—and the men who love them—are not eager to disfigure, shrink, or remove a breast. As treatment for breast cancer has evolved, women have become less willing to let zealous surgeons perform full mastectomies. Research appears to show that often the removal of just the cancerous tissue by lumpectomy, usually followed by other treatments such as chemotherapy or radiation, provides as good a prognosis as taking the entire breast. And the woman does not have to deal with as much heartache.

Ever the fighter, Racinda had already told me she wanted the best possible shot at saving her life—the breast be hanged, if keeping it meant reducing her odds. I agreed. For me this would have been a much more sobering prospect if a double mastectomy was prescribed. But all evidence thus far indicated that her other breast was in perfect health.

Some of the stories we've heard about how husbands respond to loss of a wife's breast are astonishing. One woman with a sizable breast tumor supposedly had her husband say that he would divorce her if she had a mastectomy. What a jerk! I can imagine the reception he received the next time he snuggled in for a little "lovey time" with his mate thinking, *This guy must really love me. He'd rather see me die than give up his fondling fun.*

The longer we listened, the clearer it became that the surgeon really believed Racinda's breast must be removed. She told us of a technique called TRAM flap, a surgical procedure that involves moving a woman's muscle, fat, and skin from her abdomen—without severing the blood vessels—to form a replacement breast. The surgeon suggested we see a plastic surgeon to learn more.

At first Racinda wasn't too interested. Her goal was recovery, not how she looked. Less than twenty-four hours after getting the bad news, Racinda had her boots on and was ready to march against the disease. She asked the surgeon to arrange several tests that hopefully would confirm the cancer had not spread elsewhere in her body. If the outlook was good, then she would consider the additional discomfort of surgery to rebuild a breast.

I encouraged Racinda to consider the TRAM-flap procedure. She was a young, energetic woman. Somehow I couldn't see her excited about donning a false breast each morning. Plus I felt that she was so intent on fighting the cancer that she was ignoring feelings of breast loss that might surface later.

The following day we saw the plastic surgeon. After the usual drill of paperwork and brief exam, we went to the doctor's private office for an orientation. The surgeon had a vicious cold, which impaired his ability to make a compelling sales pitch. He sniffed and wheezed, dabbing his red eyes and nose with a tissue, talking with scratchy voice. He assured us that Racinda was an excellent candidate for the procedure. The TRAM flap would be done immediately following the mastectomy, while Racinda was still under general anesthesia. She would never have to see just a scar where her breast had lived. Me either.

The doctor had talent, which was revealed when he handed us an album of snapshots of his artistry with previous patients. His demeanor was that of a proud grandpa showing photos of his grandkids. The faces and identities of the women in the photos were hidden, but I had to control an urge to giggle as we thumbed through dozens of photos of women's breasts. I searched in vain through my small-talk repertoire to find appropriate words for this odd encounter. Just what do you say while viewing such a collection? It was an improbable, impossible moment.

I remained speechless, trying to pay enough attention to evaluate the man's handiwork without slipping into prurience. I did throw in a few "Hmmms" and "Very nices" to maneuver my way through the awkward conversational moment. Overall, we were very impressed with the presentation.

I did ask the obligatory "Does insurance cover this?" question, and the answer was, "Usually, yes."

Later Racinda told me she was interested in doing this procedure, and I was glad. I believed she would survive this cancer deal and had a long life ahead. So why live it always wondering if people somehow could detect that you had only one breast?

Racinda needed to decide, though, and she was still waiting for the test results that would show whether her body was "clean" of cancer. We talked things through and she asked my opinion, but we were entering a new era of decision-making. Deciding on a TRAM flap was not the same as deciding on a Trans Am. She was not choosing a new dress, couch, house, or even a career. This was her body and her life. On decisions related to her health, Racinda was the CEO and I was a junior member of the board. It bothered me some, but I knew it was right.

Just three days after the diagnosis, we made our acquaintance with the cancer doctor, the oncologist. My role was to operate our tape recorder and make sure all questions on our list were covered. The doctor examined Racinda and then sat down to talk.

We learned that cancer-fighting physicians use significant numbers of numbers. Since no known treatment guarantees eradication of breast cancer, the best a doctor can do is explain the statistical survival rates tied to the qualities of the disease found in a particular patient. Unfortunately, "good odds of surviving" bring uneasy comfort. Even if nine of ten will live, just who is the one who won't? *Could that be my wife?* Cancer patients are also staged—their cancer is assigned a level of seriousness, from Stage I to IV; the higher the number, the worse the prognosis.

We asked our questions and left, knowing better what we were facing. From the moment she saw him, Racinda was not comfortable with the doctor. Even the way he examined her, his touch wooden and mechanical, bugged her. We hadn't learned yet how important it is for a cancer patient to have total confidence in her physician. When Racinda expressed uneasiness, I relapsed and was unsupportive and minimized her intuition. I already was so weary with the complexities of cancer treatment that I didn't want the hassle of a doctor switch.

Racinda aced her tests. The lab reports showed no cancer had spread. She decided to proceed full speed with all of the treatment, including the TRAM flap breast reconstruction.

For months our family had waited for a spring-break beach vacation in Florida. Now instead of catching waves and rays, we would all go to the hospital for Racinda's surgery. I called the Florida resort and the airline, and with my promise to provide a "written excuse" from the surgeon, received refunds. Unwilling to surrender all delight to cancer, I scrambled for an optional idea, some way to get out of town for at least a weekend of relief from the gloom.

Since we all had wanted to flee winter's chill, I calculated how far south we could drive in about six hours. Santa Fe qualified. I booked a hotel with a heated pool and we departed late on Friday afternoon.

From the time the kids could travel well (i.e., with bladder capacity for more than one rest stop on the interstate), we had enjoyed these family expeditions. Life simplifies on the road: There's a clear destination; life's necessities are in the trunk. Left behind are the hassles of work, bills, dripping faucets, and strained relationships. Best of all, family members are confined, unable to scatter to the four winds. In the car heading down the highway, in theory at least, we will talk and laugh and enjoy one another.

This would not be one of those trips. The road was straight and smooth, and on a starlit night the grassy steppe of northern New Mexico appeared a calm, endless sea. We rode in harmony, but a hostile stranger had sneaked aboard, a stowaway lurking amid the cargo of a thousand happy highway memories. Cancer was not like the usual mundane problems ditched when I pointed the prow of the family wagon to the open road.

Late that evening in Santa Fe, we found our hotel after several rotations of the narrow streets near the old-world city square. The hotel was old, but our room was charming and spotless, bringing a familiar spark to Racinda's eyes. We surrendered to our weariness and slept long and hard.

The next morning the sun shone and the temperature climbed, edging just high enough for sunbathing and refreshing dunks in the pool. This wasn't a south Florida beach, but under the circumstances we were thankful for the healing from the southwestern sun.

During breaks from the pool we explored the shops and sites of old Santa Fe. At one store I became enamored with a hat. Racinda urged me to buy it, and for the remainder of the weekend I strolled in my new broad-brimmed hat, secretly wishing perhaps a new appearance would cancel out the old troubling realities.

We tried to be the happy, on-holiday family of the past, but nothing quite sparked our dampened spirits. Was this attempt at merriment a good idea? I don't know—perhaps it did help speed the hours of waiting for the surgeons' scalpels and the pathology report on Racinda's lymph nodes.

Around noon on Sunday we climbed into the car and retraced our way north, seeing in daylight the snow-capped peaks to the west and the dry expanse of plains. The brown barrenness in all directions matched well the dusty arroyos in my heart. No longer in sight were the familiar oases, the green, moist havens of old certainties now shriveled by a desert wind.

8

_

Peach Pits

March 1997

YOU REACH A POINT where you can't put off making the call any longer. You're weary of meandering sweet talk and negotiating. It's time to give a piece of your mind.

"Hello. It's me! Just what do _You_ think You're doing? Have we done something awful to deserve _this_?"

And, as always, God listens but may wait to reply.

Now weeks into our ordeal, I noticed my spiritual platitudes had warts. I realized I must have cut class the day the prof covered "When Bad Things Happen." God seemed more likable and comprehensible when life was good.

I wasn't alone in my disorientation. Others scrambled for tight spiritual sound bites. Some said, "This has to be the devil's work." Others said, "God has a good reason for this trial."

Although I knew the intentions were kind, the nice-sounding spiritual sentiments left me the most empty. Too glib explanations made God seem limited, and I desperately needed Him to be limitless. I barely had enough strength to trust. If I had to figure Him out, too, then I was back to shouldering an enormous weight, one my trembling frame and wavering heart couldn't bear.

Surprisingly, I found more comfort in less certainty—in *mystery*, clinging to a Big Good God of perspective who knows best what is needed and when I should have answers to my prayers.

But if some of the words spoken were unsettling, the touch was divine. We were overwhelmed with kindness through delivered meals, favors, and concern. And prayer, much prayer.

The night before Racinda's surgery, pastors and others from our church came to pray. As a result of the remarkable networking of Jesus' people, prayers for Racinda's health and our family were rising throughout America and even abroad. Most of these people we didn't know and won't know. It was gratifying and humbling to realize that strangers would schedule appointments with God to plead for us.

As these friends gathered on surgery eve, Racinda and I shared the good news and bad news surrounding her situation. All tests to date had been negative. But the critical node test would reveal what the body might know and the doctors didn't.

So again we placed our destiny in capable hands. The fellow priests surrounded Racinda and laid hands upon her, advocates approaching the bar of heaven. As the sweet incense of prayer rose in our living room, my tears of relief, peace, and thanksgiving rolled in storm-swollen streams.

The surgery was scheduled for early Wednesday morning, March 26. During this two-stage operation, first the general surgeon would remove Racinda's breast and collect the lymph node sample. Next the plastic surgeon would construct a replacement breast using the TRAM-flap procedure.

After visiting with both surgeons and the anesthesiologist, Racinda and I kissed and said our good-bye in pre-op. I went to the waiting room, where several friends joined me to help pass time during the four-plus-hour operation. In time Noelle and Allan came too.

The minutes dribbled away, broken only by the spasmodic, random conversation of the surgery waiting room. Your small talk receives a concentration required for chewing gum, as your mind sees your loved one on a table under lights, instruments clanking, monitors beeping, masked, robed, gloved doctors and nurses at work. I pictured the doctor's scalpel cutting delicate tissue, precise strokes slicing away at my wife's identity. I wondered how a woman felt losing a part of herself that in puberty had helped her declare, "Hey, world! Look at me! I'm not just a little girl anymore."

In the days after the surgery, Racinda and I didn't talk much about the loss of her breast; we had too many challenges of recovery and treatment to face. But once she said to me of the missing breast, a wistful hint of loss in her voice, "That was your favorite one."

Hours later both doctors stopped in the waiting room to offer a thumbs-up on the two separate procedures. The surgeon noted that results on the node removal from Racinda's armpit would come from the pathologist in a day or two. The plastic surgeon predicted Racinda would remain comfortable as a steady flow of medication eased the pain of the ten-inch incision in her abdomen.

After Racinda recouped in the recovery room, a nurse called the children and me and we walked alongside as Racinda was rolled to her room in another wing of the hospital.

Numbed by the pain medicine, Racinda slept, occasionally rousing with a moan to ask for ice chips.

The kids left for home and in the evening a recliner was wheeled in for me—Racinda had insisted I spend at least the first night with her. I slept poorly, rousing when nurses entered or when Racinda asked for a drink or ice.

By morning she was more awake, more aware of pain. The children arrived, and as the hours ticked by, my apprehension grew about the pathologist's report. After noon I called the doctor's office—"No word yet."

This was a critical moment in our cancer battle. If cancer cells were not in the sample nodes, then Racinda would remain classified as Stage I. After the chemotherapy her statistical prognosis would be very positive. But if some of the nodes were cancer-polluted, she would drop to Stage II or worse and a more grim outlook.

Late that afternoon the phone rang. "Great news!" our always-cheerful surgeon said. "All the nodes were clean."

I announced the news to the others, and we all yelped with joy as Racinda beamed. A ray of light had pierced our family's fog.

Each day Racinda slowly regrouped. The mastectomy was nearly painless, but not so her stomach wound. She worked to regain strength, eating what she could, using a tube apparatus to exercise her lungs, and finally rising from bed to take agonizing steps.

Our overworked nurses were competent, helpful, and upbeat. One night, however, a lady came on duty who would not be my nominee for any Florence Nightingale award. Racinda already had determined that people send out either positive or negative vibes around cancer patients, and she avoided anyone who might be prone to use the words *cancer* and *death* interchangeably.

During the deep hours of the night, this nurse, who was perfectly suited for the graveyard shift, slid into our room. Instead of just checking blood pressure, pulse, and catheter bag, this sad, sunken lady also told stories—not inspiring anecdotes of healing, but grim tales of those who had suffered and died. Her spirit was gray and grimy. After one too many of her chilling visits, we turned out the lights and agreed not to ring the call button unless desperate. Whenever the nurse of despair entered the room, Racinda feigned heavy sleep and I rose like a marine on guard duty to intercept and usher her out.

By Saturday the doctors agreed Racinda could exit the hospital the next day, Easter Sunday. A friend who is a nurse and her husband arrived to help us haul Racinda and her flowers and plants home. Before discharge we were briefed on how to change the dressing on a chest catheter through which the chemotherapy drugs later would flow. Also, small drainage bottles attached to her stomach incision would occasionally need emptying. This was my first of many orientations to come on how I could be a home nurse and care for my ailing spouse.

While seeking a cancer cure, scientists have collected extensive data on the disease. The size of the tumor, the appearance of the cancer cells, the number (if any) of malignant nodes found—many factors are plugged into a huge database and a specific report is generated for the patient. Based on the details of her situation, the oncologist gave Racinda a neatly printed graph showing her outlook, depending on treatment options selected. The doctor delivered this information sensitively, but it still seemed like a bizarre, morbid sales presentation: "Since you selected the mastectomy model, if you choose chemotherapy and tamoxifen options, you have a 90 percent chance that the disease will not reoccur in a five-year period. If you choose to do nothing, the statistical odds are about 80 percent that your cancer will not return in five years."

The reality is that no matter how much treatment you buy, the odds against the cancer reappearing never reach 100 percent. And, of course, statistical odds are not guarantees. Even if your statistical profile is 99 percent positive, you still might end up in the 1 percent negative group. That's why cancer is the most hated and feared disease.

Recovering at home with time on her hands, Racinda continued to study cancer prevention. Her growing knowledge of the disease even made her wonder if she was doing the right thing in treating cancer with traditional medicine. Almost every day she stumbled upon new, usually conflicting information that forced her to reevaluate her decisions. Since no honest doctor guarantees a cancer cure, the world is full of often-desperate cancer patients eager to find someone offering a more confident prognosis.

This stage in Racinda's cancer journey, where alternative cancer treatments were under study, I soon (in the privacy of my own mind) labeled "peach pits." It was a wild, never-a-dull-moment adventure. One day Racinda would be impressed by the claims of an institution offering a body-cleansing process. The next day an extreme vegetarian diet seemed the way to go. Consideration was given clinics in other states that were experimenting with combinations of traditional medicine and alternative therapies—all very expensive. And we heard the incredible stories, from friends and strangers, of near resurrections from cancer in clinics just south of the border.

The daily possible redirections in the battle strategy were annoying, even maddening. With cancer our common enemy, our relational fussing had gone on hold. But this was a dangerous time for us—the air was full of tension, which often sparks conflict. Without divine protection our marriage could easily have blown to bits. I realized finally that Racinda needed to find her own comfort zone in facing a life threat. This thrashing through treatment options was overly emotional, but if I horned in aggressively, we would fight—and more stress we didn't need.

So I tightened the lashes on my tongue, anesthetized my facial expressions, watched my body language when receiving the daily bulletin on "peach pits." And how could I know, anyway, what might be the magic bullet of a cancer cure? Racinda deserved the freedom to fine-tune her treatment plan, as well as any diet and lifestyle changes.

We did visit some interesting health providers and heard ideas that make a spine quiver. I knew these people could not prove their claims. But I trooped along, listened, controlled my face, took notes, and prayed that Racinda would find the right path through the cancer maze.

In time she concluded that she would stick with the chemotherapy, but as her strength returned she would change her diet radically, commit herself to exercise, and find a regimen of vitamins and supplements that would bolster her immune system's ability to beat breast cancer. Made sense to me.

And she also bought a juicer—a machine that looked and sounded robust enough to extract pure, health-giving juice from tree stumps.

About a month after surgery, Racinda was judged recovered enough by the plastic surgeon to proceed with chemotherapy.

Like most everyone else, over the years in my imagination I had drawn my own picture of chemotherapy. Our oncologist and his staff had explained well the vast improvements in controlling chemotherapy side effects, but I still had old images burned into my brain cells: vomiting, baldness, sunken eyes, pale skin, mouth sores, shakiness—the look of pre-death.

Before receiving chemotherapy, Racinda would have her blood counts checked and confer with the doctor. We arrived at the clinic early one morning and waited with other patients. Racinda looked younger than most of the others. Some of the women wore hats or scarves, a clue of hair loss. Most of the men going chemo-bald left their skulls naked. Many patients appeared healthy, but there were always some slumped in chairs who looked battle-worn and weary. The chemo ward was the "front" of the cancer war.

We saw the doctor and he cleared Racinda for her first treatment. A nurse walked us to the chemotherapy area, a long room with two rows of stuffed recliners. At one end was a small kitchen stocked with beverages, crackers, and other snacks. Two tables held partially completed jigsaw puzzles. A TV flickered and squawked in a corner. Racinda chose a chair facing the windows, and I sat down nearby.

Cancer nurses are lion souls. How else could they survive this day after day? Our nurse was warm and engaging. While efficiently stringing up several chemical bags on an IV pole, she learned the facts about our kids, Racinda's job, and other tidbits of family history. She wove me into the chatter, too, prodding my spirits with good-natured jabs.

The first part of the treatment was the intravenous infusion of anti-nausea medication. Next would come the bags of two chemo drugs. The whole process would take about two hours. Racinda was soon hooked up via her chest catheter; we now saw how this ingenious gizmo meant the chemo poison would not have to run through a needle into her arm. With the steady drip-drip-drip under way, the nurse whizzed off to other patients, all at various stages of the day's encounter with chemotherapy.

I looked at the others and was gratified to note that my fears might not materialize—no one was moaning or puking. Racinda and I turned our attention to books and magazines and settled in.

The nurse came again and switched Racinda to the first bag. I watched the drug called Cytoxan drain into her body. So far so good; she didn't feel much of anything. The second bag, its contents the rust-colored Adriamycin, also flowed without incident.

The nurse unhooked the tubes, asked how Racinda felt, and then let us go.

We drove home and Racinda rested. In case they were needed, anti-nausea pills were prescribed, but she never felt very sick. After a day or two the fatigue lifted and she resumed normal activities.

Maybe this chemo deal wasn't so bad after all.

Yes, on some of the darker days, I wanted to run. Not to slip off in the night on a Harley Davidson or to catch a freighter to New Zealand, but to distance myself from this ugly, entangling disease that threatened to suck us both into a pit and ruin everything. I hated that our lives had changed. I feared the pain, too. So I encountered the temptation to unhook emotional lines connecting me to Racinda.

Another force was at work, though. In my gaze was a precious human being who happened to be my wife . . . and she really needed me. No place now for charades or facades, for the mental one-upmanship to decide who was holding the best hand in our marital game. My promise had come due—to stand steady in sickness and health.

As I walked with Racinda through the dark valley, love taught a new lesson. This was not grim duty but joyful privilege—to listen, to help lift her burden, to encourage another

eternal soul, to even feel—because of our sacred oneness—
that I, too, bore the disease.

To my shame, it had taken the threat of losing her to know
that I could not bear the thought of losing her.

Temptations to flee passed. The only place I wanted to run
was close, very close.

Does every woman in chemotherapy believe she might be the
one not to lose her hair? Racinda had spoken with other cancer warriors and done reading to determine her chances of
skipping the shiny head look. The outlook was disappointing:
One of Racinda's chemotherapy drugs, Adriamycin, virtually
guaranteed hair loss. But one friend had used vitamins with
success, and supposedly a certain brand of shampoo was effec-
tive. So Racinda used both.

And to hedge her bets, she bought a wig that resembled her
most recent cut. The wig, which came with a bald mannequin
for storage, was parked on a shelf in the master bathroom.

The purpose of chemotherapy is to kill fast-growing cells,
like the cancer freak ones. But the chemo does not differenti-
ate between good and bad fast-growing cells. Since the cells
that produce hair are rapid growing, a good dose of most chemo
drugs is followed in about three weeks by gradual—or rapid—
hair loss.

For more than a week Racinda's hair held firm. Then more
hair than normal stuck in her comb. Strands of hair decorated

the pillowcase in the morning. After her shower, hair littered the bottom of the stall. For a while the missing hair was not noticeable. But then bald spots appeared and a general thinning began. In spite of shampoo, vitamins, and cautious combing, hair dropped in bunches. One morning I awoke with strands of her hair in my mouth.

Racinda kept the resilient locks as long as she could but always wore a hat in public. At home, though, not concerned that her scalp looked like the occasional stalks of grass in a newly sprouted lawn, she went head nude. Finally tired of finding shed hair everywhere, she gave up and commissioned Allan to use the electric clippers and give her a marine boot-camp special. After several low passes of the trimmer, all hair was gone.

And it wasn't just hair on her scalp that departed. Soon there was no need to shave legs, and even eyebrows and eyelashes began to disappear.

When Racinda went to the grocery store or elsewhere, she put on the wig. Those outside our family did not know this was fake hair, and many people wear wigs all the time. But Racinda hated the wig and all the pain, fear, and frustration—the interruption of her life it symbolized. She wore it not a second longer than needed, often lifting it quickly as soon as we closed the car doors. And when Racinda was at home, the wig knew its place, warming the mannequin's Styrofoam skull in the bathroom.

I struggled to understand the anger and loss she felt concerning her hair. Keeping every strand in perfect place had never been Racinda's focus as she zipped through her days. Why was this hair thing such a big deal? Eventually I realized that a woman's hair is the finishing touch on the presentation of her self to the world—the crown of her beauty. And her hair is a covering, too, an elegant cloth concealing nakedness. Hairlessness implied humiliation and shame.

And I ached so for her. Other scars of her cancer battle were concealed, but only a lifeless, itchy, despised wig could help hide the absence of living, growing, flowing hair. How do you convince yourself and others that life is okay when in the mirror you see a bald head, smooth and shiny as a cue ball?

The chemo treatments occurred every three weeks, but after the first one, Racinda asked for a delay, since the second would fall just days before Noelle's high school graduation. The doctor agreed, and we moved our attention from the disease to this happy moment in our daughter's life. Plans for the graduation party were made and relatives arrived from out of town.

On a Saturday morning we sat in the packed gymnasium and cheered as Noelle waved, diploma in hand. Afterward we posed for pictures, arms around each other, smiling brightly.

I look at those photos now and smile at details a casual eye will never see. Standing near me in the Kodak moment, smiling, is the love of my life. Her electric blue dress conceals the chemotherapy catheter held by a dressing I sometimes changed, as well as the angry scar on her stomach that prevented her bending to tie her shoes. Atop her head is a white, broad-brimmed hat, largely concealing lush locks of jet black hair—the hated wig (its time is short; soon we would be in the car). Behind Racinda's glasses I see just shadows of once bold brows.

Only I can see these things; to others glancing at Racinda and Bruce's world, this is the perfect picture of a joy-filled moment.

And it was a day of joy . . . and a day of sadness. Another day on the journey.

9

Was That Just a Bad Dream?

Summer 1997

IN JULY, A WEEK BEFORE the last of Racinda's four chemotherapy treatments, the two of us drove to North Dakota for
my high school reunion.

Before we left, her white blood count was low as a result
of the previous treatment. She felt fine, but the deficiency
reduced the ability of her immune system to fight infection.
The doctor warned us to be cautious but gave permission for
the trip.

Just the two of us on a car trip alone—this was odd. The
kids, busy with jobs, friends, and the latest movies, no longer
were subcontractors on call to their parental architects.

On the road we remembered the time when it was just
us—making our schedule on the fly, doing "our thing." As the
car hummed across the reaches of Nebraska, bugs splattering
in Technicolor on the windshield, Racinda and I caught up on
topics ignored for months during the cancer ordeal. We dined

on food and drink from a backseat cooler. Eating choices would be adjusted on this trip.

With treatment nearly complete, Racinda's mind-set on the cancer was proactive: If there was anything that might help prevent a recurrence, she would try it. Her old diet was one of the first casualties of the before-cancer life.

This pained me because I liked what I ate. The family menu had evolved from the full-fat to the low-fat approach—that was okay. We ate more chickens than cows and had fruits and veggies most meals. I'd never met a cheese-laden casserole, sweet roll, bread, brownie, cookie, pie, or cake for which I didn't feel rapport. What was wrong with solid Midwestern farm fare?

Not too much—until cancer showed up.

Racinda was convinced that diet plays a leading role in breast cancer. She did not ask the rest of the family to abandon nearly all meat and milk products, but her enthusiasm for turning out the good old meals was gone.

Before long we were shopping for groceries in a store that seemed more New Age cathedral than market. The organic goods were healthy, but on early visits I gagged on the incense.

The store definitely had ambience and flair. One entire section held rows of bottles of natural pills and potions with names like Bladderwrack and Bugleweed Motherwort Supreme. A book section included titles like *The Tofu Tollbooth, Tissue Cleansing Through Bowel Management,* and *Treat Your Face Like a Salad.* I couldn't find fried chicken in the deli, but they had plenty of Saag Baag and tofu burritos. The employees were the most intriguing aspect, friendly and mostly young people apparently frozen in time during the sixties and revived thirty years later. The hair, the clothes, the tie-dye, the relaxed perspective—this was, like man, hippieville.

Racinda's wholesale diet change triggered mourning for me. I realized fast how much junk food meant to me. I didn't begrudge Racinda's desire to use new food and preparation techniques as a weapon against disease. But I grieved that we would no longer go together for barbecue and beans or even freely accept dinner invitations from friends. And what might it be like inviting guests to our home for culinary cruises featuring tofu and curd?

As it turned out, I was overreacting. But beating this fear of losing my food was another unexpected and troubling twist in our cancer experience.

I did not starve on the way to North Dakota. We found restaurants that offered some menu items Racinda deemed healthy, and in a pinch even at a fast-food trough, while I dived for a burger, she found a salad or baked potato.

After a visit with my brother and wife in Fargo, on Saturday morning we set out on my journey to yesterday. I had not seen my boyhood scenes for more than twenty-five years, and Racinda had never visited North Dakota. I had much to show and tell her.

Reunion activities were not scheduled until the afternoon,

so we went sightseeing. There wasn't much to look at. On the farm where I'd first lived, the place that had neither electricity nor running water in my early childhood, every building had collapsed or been relocated. These ghost farms are everywhere in North Dakota, remnants of the death of rural family enterprise.

At the second farm we could see that only two buildings remained. Knee-high grass covered the lane from the main road to the farmstead, so Racinda—already dressed for the evening banquet—stayed in the car. I took my camera and hiked in, passing a familiar grove of trees. The yard that had seemed enormous in childhood now looked tiny. Only charred wood and crumbling basement walls marked the remains of our house. A mysterious fire had claimed it years before. The barn, where many a summer day was spent pitching decayed sheep manure, was just a pile of rotting boards. It had tumbled in a windstorm.

The garage still stood, and inside, an oil-stained workbench held the same rusting bolts and broken tools I'd known thirty years ago. Cobwebs curtained dirty windows. In a corner I found a blue fender from my first bike. I decided to take it as a souvenir of my childhood.

After snapping pictures, I walked to the car. These ruins hardly resembled a home filled with oven smells and Mother's laugh. Gone were the blooming flowers, the ragged dogs and cats, the trimmed lawn used for family croquet matches. I returned to Racinda damp from the humidity and with wood ticks ascending my pantleg. We drove off, and I won't need to go back.

In Cooperstown, the small town where I was born, we finally found a surviving landmark I could show Racinda, the small Bethlehem church with parsonage next door, still painted yellow after all these years.

We drove several streets, trying to jar my memory to recall the small house where the midwife had delivered me. I stopped to ask directions and learned the house had been moved—not exactly sure where.

So we drove back toward the reunion site, with me thinking that the prairie in North Dakota is fighting back, a revolution to restore the land to sod. How else can you explain the demise of places I'd cherished? In another decade or two, will all traces that I ever existed amid the windblown grass be gone?

The class reunion began with a reception at mid-afternoon. Since this was an all-class homecoming tied to the town of Finley's centennial, several classes were assigned to the same room to reconnect, which made matching old names with unrecognizable faces more challenging. I'd not seen most of these people for more than thirty years, a long time for nature to erode the human body. Thank goodness for name tags, but some people were not wearing them. Confusion reigned.

One distinguished older man (everyone looked *very* old) greeted me excitedly, pumping my hand, speaking fondly of experiences we'd shared. My long-lost buddy—I had not a clue who he was. Others no doubt scrambled through mind closets when looking at my face. It was bizarre, unnerving, hilarious.

Eerily, even after all these years, the high school pecking order was undisturbed. If the school bell had chimed, immediately we would have taken our assigned seats in the social order. The hotshots of yore had not lost their swagger. Nor had I lost my furious envy.

As the day wore on, I noted how the popular dream girls had fared. Several of the cuter ones made no appearance. Girls, and boys, too, were packing more weight and wrinkles, which obscured their past loveliness. My memories of teenage longing for these beauties slipped with ease from mental mothballs. In high school my self-esteem hadn't allowed much more than thinking about girls. But now, a mature, experienced man of the world, obviously in his prime—might not I actually catch a wistful smile from one of the goddesses?

This fantasy fell as flat as those I'd had back when I'd tilled an acne farm on my face.

The evening banquet was in the gym, site of basketball games, plays, band concerts, and graduation. While devouring mounds of chicken and beef, we reviewed the funny and poignant memories. The program ended, and we former pals made promises to stay in touch that we'd not kept before and won't again.

Racinda and I drove off, she shedding her wig at the town limits, I shedding moldy notions that life back then had a special shine. Memories, both bad and good, are overrated. We earth pilgrims are designed for the now. It's the evil spoiler who teases us to pine for days gone or yet to be.

The last drop of the chemotherapy juice trickled into Racinda's catheter on July 8. On the way home we stopped to celebrate with her favorite "sinful" treat, McDonald's vanilla low-fat yogurt. This was the moment long awaited—now life could turn back toward normal—whatever that might be P.B.C. (post–breast cancer).

Racinda was energetic enough to return to work, so the annual push to prepare for opening day at the elementary school began. In mid-August we transported Noelle and a van full of stuff to her college near Chicago. After several days of orientation, I faced the long-dreaded good-bye to the second most important woman in my life. This was raw pain. We took pictures in front of her dormitory and had a final family group hug. Then with the tears falling like rain, we ripped ourselves away, climbed in the van, and drove off. There she stood, waving, eyes wet. The only good thing about this moment is that I'll never have to endure one exactly like it again.

Our routine resumed. On weekdays Racinda and Allan left early for school, after which I usually paused to read my Bible, ponder life, and pray. After giving a final wave to Nala, golden retriever in residence, I took the downstairs commute to the basement for another day of sentence assembly.

Were these days really the same as the good old days? I didn't sit myself down and ask, "Now Bruce, how have the events of recent months—facing the life-threatening disease of your wife and the nest exit of your only daughter—affected you? How are you *really* doing, big fella?" No, in typical male, stoic Swede fashion, I assumed that since Racinda was back on track and I had shed my tears several weeks ago in Chicago, all was well in Bruceworld. Only after wandering around under a cloud for weeks did it dawn on me that something wasn't right. So then I sat down on my couch and realized I was suffering some peacetime letdown. The cancer battle was over. No more bullets snapping over my head. No need to plan the next counterattack. My adrenaline battery was switched off. And I was tired, empty, and drained of enthusiasm.

In time I reached peace concerning the unsettling aspects of our new life. Racinda didn't force me to eat her new food, we still could go to restaurants with friends, and the e-mail from our departed daughter filled some of the void.

And slowly, normal returned. Racinda's diet and exercise routine had her slimmer and stronger. Her hair grew back, from a blonde fuzz, to black sprouts, to curly locks. The wig was stored and Racinda went topless—no hat. Through wizardry in separate surgical procedures, the plastic surgeon gave Racinda's reconstructed breast a fake nipple and even an areola (the pigmented area around the nipple) via tattoo.

The chemotherapy had rushed Racinda through menopause. Her spirits were good.

With each day of regained health, the memory of the bad cancer days dimmed. *Had all of that really happened or was it just a bad dream? Was the crisis over for good?*

Oh, if only it were that easy. In time the fear of cancer subsides. But to experience a disease like this is to surrender the naïve notion that no harm will ever befall you.

Like most cancer warriors Racinda monitored her body as never before. Any ache or pain or pressure or irregularity anywhere was noted, analyzed, and declared a candidate for fear. We noncombatants may fuss and complain about symptoms, but we do not know what it's like to have both the ache in the leg as well as the dread that this might be the sign the cancer is back.

And it's not just messages from your own body that trigger fear. The cancer survivor arises rested and recharged on a fine morning, but on the breakfast table the newspaper may bear a story of the actress, the philanthropist, the beloved mother of a politician who "yesterday lost her fight with breast cancer." And a cool wind chills the spirit.

Or on the job a coworker may catch you at the coffee station and report in hushed, sad tones, "I just found out that one of my best friends in high school found a tumor the size of an egg in her breast—and it's *cancer!*" Then with a shake of the head the bearer of such tidings slinks away to her desk, leaving the breast cancer survivor with a boiling brew of emotions—empathy, sorrow, anger, confusion, and fear.

Racinda developed weapons to shield herself from such

"friendly fire." As much as possible she avoided people who carried the pessimism virus. And she learned to consume cancer news but not to overindulge. When even her best defenses were penetrated with an unsettling cancer message, she would "sit herself down" and recite like a creed the facts of her own case, recalling the good news and answered prayers concerning her health. And finally she would surrender—acknowledging, as we all must, that the days and events of her life were not in her own hands but in the scarred, loving hands of One who had promised never to leave or forsake her.

In October, after much agonizing, Racinda changed doctors. Her nagging discomfort with the original oncologist never subsided. The switch was a good thing to do. On top of all the physical and emotional crud that accompanies cancer, you don't need to add the anxiety of distrusting the physician who's trying to keep you alive.

The change was stressful. She didn't want to hurt the first doctor's feelings or create some backlash at the clinic against her. But the switch of doctors was no big deal; no angry call came from a heartbroken cancer doc. We learned that breast cancer patients frequently try more than one doctor before finding the desired rapport and trust.

Slowly life did ease toward normalcy—different but pleasantly predictable. The significant exceptions were the weeks when a doctor's visit was scheduled. It didn't matter how good

Racinda felt, in the days before the blood draw and the evaluation with the doctor, an anxiousness grew in us both. Then the doctor would report, "The blood work is fine" (*Whew! Relief number one*), and after carefully probing the breasts and lymph glands with well-trained fingers and listening through the stethoscope, would issue the final benediction: "You look great; see you in three months" (*Yeah! Relief number two*).

The 1998 holidays came and went. The children—based on the day's events—continued the cycle of euphoria and despair. Work crises crested and abated. Life was life again.

Racinda celebrated her first cancer-free year anniversary by planting a pine tree in the yard. She planned to do this every year, and I liked the idea of our lot some day looking like a national forest. The rigors of fighting cancer together had first distracted us from dwelling on our problems, then shaped up some parts of our relationship.

I wanted to believe that the storm had passed, and acted accordingly. Maybe we could sigh contentedly at day's end and put our heads on the pillow to find dreams instead of nightmares.

10

Counterattack

May 1998

IT HAD BEEN A PRODUCTIVE WEEK. On a warm Friday afternoon in May, I was completing work tasks in my home office. A golf round was tee-timed for later, and I was savoring having our daughter home after her freshman year of college. Noelle had not started a summer job, so she had offered to go with her mom to a routine visit with the oncologist.

Summer beckoned brightly for the family—no cancer this year. Racinda was particularly expectant. She felt great and had the energy to tackle a list of postponed activities during her break from teaching.

At about 4:00 P.M. I heard footsteps descending the stairway and approaching my office. Our confident hopes and best-laid plans were about to crumble.

The door swung open. It was Racinda, cheeks wet with tears. "The doctor found a lump under my arm!" she said, her words a mixture of hurt, fear, and disbelief.

I slumped in my chair, but even as my dread rose, I assumed my combat officer role. I asked questions, learning the hopeful news that the doctor had said this was "probably nothing, but you better have your surgeon check it out."

"Probably nothing" didn't fill me with much confidence, but as Racinda reported on the oncologist's response, she expressed agreement with this outlook.

"I really don't think there's anything to this," she said with a hint of bravado. She did feel great, the blood work just done was perfect, her diet and exercise regimen had her in fantastic shape—how could she have cancer *again?*

But here we were, caught once more on a Friday afternoon with a list of questions and no one available with answers until next week. I did not like the way this felt.

We had learned the first time around that many people freak out when they hear the word *cancer.* And hysteria worsens if news spreads that "her cancer might be back!" Since we didn't know what that little lump under Racinda's arm was, we only told a few friends. If the lump was benign, we would not have to track down rumors. Just in case, though, we rolled the big prayer guns out of the armory and fired some practice rounds.

On Sunday afternoon, while I was passing some time, struggling to keep anxiety on a tight leash, a friend called and asked, "Did you hear about Brent?"

I hadn't heard a word about my soul mentor-counselor for a long time.

"No . . . what's up?"

"He died yesterday in a climbing accident. He was about to reattach his safety line when he lost his balance and went over a cliff."

We talked for a few more minutes, but I didn't react to the tragic news. I hung up and wished I could muster some grief pain or shed tears, but I was dry. The small cup of emotional juice I'd stored in recent months was draining low due to my own looming crisis. I did feel loneliness. No more Brent on call if I needed him. No soul sage to field questions I hadn't even thought of yet. He had died during a men's wilderness retreat, still a Moses leading other wandering brothers from desert to the promised land.

Man, I would miss him.

*

On Monday we saw the surgeon, and a biopsy was scheduled for the next day.

The following morning Racinda once again went through the same pre-op drill at the same hospital, then rode off to surgery on a kiss and a prayer. Within an hour the surgeon arrived in the waiting room. I knew her lines before she spoke them—"It went well." But then she abandoned the script. "I found two swollen lymph nodes and removed them both.

They have gone to pathology. I think we'll have the report tomorrow." I gave her my phone number.

Next she ruined my day. "Keep saying your prayers," she said.

I knew then we were toast. This most optimistic and cheerful of doctors, like a weatherman whose skies are never partly cloudy but always partly sunny, had come close to forecasting rain. Just what miserable tissue had her scalpel encountered?

Racinda and I drove home. I didn't tell her of the surgeon's religious instruction. We were praying plenty anyway.

The next morning Racinda returned to her job. She hadn't told anyone at work about the latest incident, wishing the status of a healthy person as long as there was no contrary evidence.

I, too, escaped into tasks, although the combat officer in my brain had set up a war room and was rehearsing "What if?" contingencies.

Racinda called during a break: "Any word yet?"

"No."

A former work associate called, wanting to ensure I knew of Brent's death and the funeral, which would occur in a few hours. Without saying why, I told her I would not attend. Innocently, she inquired about Racinda's health, and maintaining to the ludicrous end our cover story, I babbled on about how great she felt, the superb doctor reports, blah-blah-blah.

Just seconds after I said good-bye, the surgeon's call came.

"I have bad news. The nodes were cancerous."

And while the doctor and I were still on the phone, I heard the call waiting signal and knew it was Racinda. I was not ready to put a gun to the head of her last hope that this last week was just a passing shadow. So I ignored the beep.

The doctor got off the line, and I sat alone and empty. In seconds the phone rang again. Of course Racinda knew I hadn't answered because I was talking to the surgeon: "Tell me what she said," she prompted, her voice shrill with fear.

I wanted to lie, to tell some fairy tale of elves and pumpkins and wands. But I was in a corner and had no room to maneuver such a deception. So I told her. No matter how kind the delivery of such a message, you feel the knife plunging into the heart.

"I can't believe it," she said and cried.

"I'm sorry, honey. I'll pick you up in a few minutes."

The truce was over. We were back at war.

The next morning we arrived early at the oncology clinic, waiting again with the other cancer battlers, everyone wondering how serious the wounds of the others.

A nurse of good cheer weighed Racinda in, as always sharing joyful words, and then parked us in the examining room. While Racinda undressed and slipped on the paper gown, I readied the tape recorder and reviewed our notes. Today I was an investigative reporter.

We were clueless as to what treatment the doctor might

recommend. A cancer recurrence in the axillary—armpit—nodes is rare, happening in less than 5 percent of all cases. Our revered cancer resource, *Dr. Susan Love's Breast Book*, appeared to suggest that a disease rerun like this was not a big deal. Maybe the oncologist would propose a few radiation treatments or even conclude that the surgical removal of the nodes had done the trick. We both hoped fervently that additional chemotherapy would be unnecessary, mainly because of the hair-loss thing.

After the obligatory exam and Racinda was dressed, the oncologist came back and gave his lecture. The doctor acknowledged that Racinda's situation was rare and puzzling, but a recurrence in the nodes was much preferred to a cancer attack of the bones or organs elsewhere in the body. Yet any recurrence was not good.

"So what do you propose to do?" I asked.

And a day that was already gray turned black.

The doctor proposed a three-stage treatment plan, based on the assumption that the cancer was localized. If tests verified Racinda was as "healthy" as he thought, then the treatment would include chemotherapy with different drugs, a bone marrow transplant (BMT), and radiation.

About halfway through his description of the BMT procedure, Racinda nearly fainted. The doctor and I helped her lie down on the examining table. He offered to leave while she regrouped, but that's not the modus operandi of a fighter. "No, keep going," she said weakly, pressing a hand against her forehead.

The doctor continued, skillfully nudging us near the abyss so we could see the danger but not moving so fast that we slipped over the edge.

Finally he stopped and asked if we had questions. While I stumbled through the fog in my mind, groping for a profound inquiry, Racinda asked if she could start those tests *today*.

The doctor said he would try to arrange them and suggested we visit with someone from the BMT unit.

Numbly we gathered our belongings and left, floating in a silent, surreal world. Shocked, I scrambled to catch a single rational thought. *What in the world was going on? Why was the doctor proposing a treatment plan that sounded like World War III?*

We stopped to speak with a nurse at the hospital's BMT unit. After introductory chitchat, the issue of insurance coverage surfaced. When we told the carrier's name, the nurse responded, "Oh, that company is kind of difficult to deal with. You can depend on it! They will refuse to cover a bone marrow transplant, and you'll have to appeal. But usually after the appeal they approve it. We would have to get to work on this right away."

Oh, joy!

Our minds whirling with questions concerning the future, we forced ourselves to focus on *the* question: Had the cancer spread elsewhere in Racinda's body? We learned that her bone and CT scans were scheduled for early afternoon. Our pastor and wife, planning to meet us for lunch anyway, picked up sandwiches and joined us at the hospital.

While they kept Racinda company, I called an oncologist in Texas who had seen Racinda on a consultation the previous summer. Without a second opinion I was not about to send my wife into hellacious treatment that could potentially kill or maim her. After several calls, arrangements were set for the following week.

Racinda had the first test and a kind attendant said at its conclusion, "The bone scan looks great. Your doctor should give you the report later today."

We went immediately for the second test and received another positive report—"All clean."

A tiny smile brightened Racinda's face. How I loved her courageous spirit. On a foreboding day, a ray of hope flickered, as it always does.

Racinda needed a brain MRI before she could decide if treatment that would scorch her immune system was worth it. And since this was Friday—a Friday before a three-day holiday weekend—once again we had to wait.

On Monday I went to my office to transcribe the tape made during the oncologist's visit and catch up on work. Near the end of the afternoon, Racinda burst into the room— "We've got to go get Allan; he's rolled the Jeep!"

"Is he okay?" I asked, my mind pleading with God— *Please, no more pain, I don't think I could bear it.*

"He says he is, but he's shook up."

Allan, now sixteen, had obtained his driver's license four months earlier. This summer he drove himself to his lawn service jobs. He was a solid driver but still learning the nuances of gas pedal and brake.

Racinda, Noelle, and I sped to the accident site, a dirt road on private property. When we arrived ten minutes later, our Jeep Cherokee was upright, sitting sideways in the middle of the road, tires flat, surrounded by puddles of shattered glass. Allan sat nearby, head down. We hugged him and checked him over. Because of his seat belt, and no doubt angels who had kept the gasoline cans from spilling and igniting an inferno, he was fine—not a scratch on his fine young frame. So we had church right there. I prayed one of those good, no holy baloney prayers: "Dear God, thank You so much for protecting Allan's life."

We called a tow truck, and I examined the accident scene. I walked back up the road seeking clues to the cause—*Had he been driving too fast?* Then I looked at the mangled vehicle. I remembered how we had dropped all but required insurance coverage on the old car. I was sure the Jeep was a goner, that we couldn't afford another car now, and how would Allan service his clients the rest of the summer? Another ache wedged in among the others in my throbbing skull.

But amid my dismal, pragmatic musings, a thought fluttered triumphantly as a phoenix: I had the most important thing, a living, whole son I could talk to and hug—a son whose life was preserved. And such basics as a breathing, healthy boy were precious these days.

The next morning I went early to the auto repair shop where the tow truck had deposited the Jeep. Some of my other wrecked cars had received healing there at low cost. The shop's owner, a man large of belly and small on words, walked around the scarred vehicle, poking and prodding, scratching his chin.

"Can you make it drivable and safe?" I asked tentatively. "It doesn't have to look pretty."

"Yeah. Nine hundred bucks."

I wanted to kiss the guy! This car was totaled. Any insurance company would laugh at the idea of fixing it.

"The frame is okay. I can tell it was a slow, soft rollover."

I told him to proceed, and as I drove away the sun was rising against the crystal blue Colorado sky, a sight to match my mood. I was a satisfied man. At last one broken thing in my little universe could be fixed!

Later that morning Racinda had the brain MRI test and the results were NED—no evidence of disease. The path was clear. If she wished, she could proceed with the chemotherapy-BMT-radiation holocaust, the medical equivalent of using nuclear warheads against a "rumored" squad of insurgent guerrillas "possibly" holed-up in a cave in a hostile country.

I laughed later in the day when I realized the irony. This was a *great* day. First I'd been delighted I could spend nine hundred bucks to put a junker car back on the road. And then the super news that my wife was healthy enough to undergo treatment that could kill her in order to save her life! To think that only weeks before my list of pre-eminent concerns included issues like straightening my errant golf swing.

Life is adept at refining crude ideas of what's important.

With a second jolt from cancer, Racinda surrendered any remaining naïveté about death's reality. Gone were smug assumptions about time. No more playing games.

Racinda looked at her life and decided she would not wait any longer to confront glitches in her thinking, emotions, and behavior that caused such pain. She wanted someone who could help her—fast. And she found the one I call the Incredible Lady—a wizened, white-haired, petite, gentle mind–artist with compassion forged of steel.

Her title was counselor, and her license proved it, but the Incredible Lady was shaped by life's rigors not for occupation but ministry, to be the hands of healing for wounded and tortured hearts.

The Incredible Lady and Racinda met at the providential crossroads. Along the way other helpers had identified the garbage in her life and even carried out a load or two, but there were far too many piles of old, useless stuff still cluttering up Racinda's otherwise tidy house.

The Incredible Lady practiced her artistry in a room of her home—a welcoming sign read, "Remove your shoes at the door, thank you!" Her unassuming demeanor belied a fervor to deliver relief from torment with haste. She was like an aggressive but wise surgeon who because of hatred for disease wants to cut out the slimy tumor *now!*

Together, the Incredible Lady and Racinda probed relational malfunctions from long ago and the warped results they had sired. With her words and expressions and gestures, using the tools of her craft and grace-given gifts, the Incredible Lady helped her daughter-on-loan find and see the child, girl, and woman God had made. Racinda learned to accept her humanity, the good and the bad. She found forgiveness and began to give it away. Hope moved in as fear packed its bags.

Broken glass was carefully arranged and glue applied.

I began to notice some change in Racinda and did not fully approve. She was happier, but her more confident outlook was unnerving. *Would this new woman still love me tomorrow?*

Since the early days of our twosome, Racinda had provided me with what amounted to an emotional landfill. Whenever I had some attitude slop, anxiety junk, or anger muck, I could head over to Racinda's landfill and dump. I did this with my controlling, clever, and often angry words.

Without my permission the Incredible Lady helped Racinda close her landfill. She gave Racinda healthy communication tools, ways to express feelings kindly but directly. She taught her how to disable controlling maneuvers. She helped her get on her emotional feet to become a partner instead of a slave.

As I always had before, I continued to drive up to Racinda's landfill with my two tons of garbage, but now the gate was chained shut. Racinda eyed my truck, flies buzzing above the foul load, and listened courteously as I explained my need to dump. But unlike the past, she would not get the key and open the landfill gate.

So I had to drive off with my smelly pile. It took a while, but I finally opened my own landfill and began creative recycling. And I actually felt good that Racinda had closed her waste disposal site and moved to another place that didn't smell so bad. Now when I visited her and we talked like friends, we didn't have the distraction of all that garbage.

Of course we still had days when for old times' sake the landfill opened up and I swung by with a full load. That's the old human sin deal. But we were making progress . . . and it was good.

11

Gunslinger Wanted

June 1998

WE JUST DID NOT KNOW what to do.

Still confused by the severity of the proposed treatment, we looked forward to a second opinion from the Texas doctor.

Two days before our trip, I stopped at a bookstore to scan the cancer section. Mixed among a hundred titles I found a book explaining the bone marrow transplant procedure. This research was for me, not for Racinda.

The book's author, a cancer patient's husband, described in graphic, agonizing detail his wife's experience. After reading bits and pieces of a few pages, I couldn't take any more descriptions of the pain-wracked frame, violent vomiting, and a chemo-devastated body slipping dangerously near death.

I tried futilely to untangle my thoughts as I drove home. On top of my fear I now had a promising case of paranoia. Our oncologist's catastrophic treatment plan made no sense to me. I was questioning whether the cancer clinic or some sinister backroom force was demanding more patient flow for the organization's BMT unit. I could not grasp why such radical treatment was necessary. And to put the icing on my anxiety, insurance might decline coverage of this expensive treatment. What a charming prospect: I possibly could watch my wife die and go bankrupt at the same time.

The potential money woes of the unfolding scenario had spread through my thoughts like a wicked virus, invading much of my conscious mental territory. Unknown to Racinda I stopped back by the BMT unit. Because the insurance was iffy, I wanted to know how much the treatment would cost and what happened if the insurer ultimately denied the claim.

The receptionist's smile faded when I blurted out my questions with a voice brittle with stress. She called a supervisor, who rushed to her rescue. I repeated my questions and got answers: "The procedure costs about $87,000, and if insurance won't pay, we need the full payment in advance."

I scrambled outdoors for fresh air. Now what was I to do? Would I be forced to choose between my wife's life and financial ruin?

Racinda and I had agreed early in the cancer journey that we would not keep secrets and hold back feelings. Now I wasn't so sure the rule applied. Honesty has a narcotic pull in a relationship, so finally I told her what I had learned, somewhat expecting this news to induce panic. But she had on her game face. There was only one struggle worthy of significant attention—her fight against the cancer. This side issue would have to wait.

"Let's not worry about it," she said. "We don't even know exactly what we're going to do, and the insurance will probably pay."

I apologized for even mentioning it, but she sternly reminded me that we were in this together. Her confidence dropped my anxiety to a manageable level, and after a few days of pleading with God for some peace, I, too, consigned the whole dilemma to the "whatever" box and focused on helping Racinda decide how to eradicate the cancer.

My recommitment to honesty wasn't total. I didn't have the stomach to tell her what I'd read about BMT in that depressing book.

&

We flew to Texas lugging not carry-on suitcases but a bundle of mammograms, bone scans, MRI film, and pathology slides. This was to be a one-day trip to compare notes on our medical advice. We both clung to a wish that this other cancer expert would study Racinda's case, wrinkle his brow, and say, "I just don't understand why your oncologist proposed such aggressive treatment. All you need is some radiation and to get on with your life!"

At the Texas clinic the receptionist took our load of films and reports. After a wait we were ushered deep into the clinic, the holy of holies where the doctor had his examining rooms.

After more waiting he bolted in and examined Racinda, then we talked. Next he rushed to consult with other doctors and we waited again. When he returned, his first sentence was exactly what we'd come a thousand miles to hear—"We can take care of this." To better explain the details, he led us to a cluttered office with a large marker board.

Like a general sketching out a three-front battle plan, the doctor drew a sizable diagram on the board. As he penciled in chemo drugs, radiation doses, and time periods, we discovered his treatment plan was a nearly twenty-four-month, multiforce assault. Racinda would receive waves of chemotherapy, culminating in a double blast of high-dose chemo and a BMT.

This was definitely Texas, land of "We do things big here." The doctor's proposal reminded me of one of those Texan pickups with a gun rack inside the rear window filled with six rifles, and "just in case," a loaded automatic pistol in the glove box.

The doctor didn't say it this way, but in Texas medical pickup talk he was giving us the equivalent of, "Sh-o-o-o-t, you gotta blow this cancer to kingdom come! If three chemo bottles are good, six'll be twice as good!"

Since a trend was emerging of aggressive response to Racinda's recurrence, we kind of liked the sound of a blow-it-away option. Cancer is a disease that makes you wish to stick a gun barrel in its face and empty six clips on full automatic—no jury trial, no appeals, no clemency talk, no writing poetry on death row—just "To the courtyard now, Dirty Cancer, and prepare to meet your doom!"

I asked this doctor of his success in obtaining insurance coverage. He snorted, "Well, they *have to pay* for the chemotherapy and radiation. Many of them refuse to pay for the high-dose chemo and transplant, but if you have to take them to court, we've never lost!" End of discussion.

Once again in the Lone Star way, without really asking what we wanted to do, the Texas cancer ranger initiated plans for Racinda's treatment, enlisting our doctor in Colorado to join the posse.

Sobered, weary, and confused, we gathered our bundle of medical documentation and flew home.

Arriving home later that evening, we picked up Noelle and Allan for a long-awaited weekend in the mountains. We drove two hours, winding in the dark up a tree-filled canyon, checked in late, and fell into an exhausted, dream-deficient sleep. It's a long way from a Texas cancer shop to a cabin in Estes Park.

The next day we hiked and golfed and ate and talked about the dire treatment scenario that could consume the next year. The reward for running this demanding track was a good chance that Racinda would win and save her life. We all clung to the reports that the disease we so "wanted dead" had been sighted only near her chest.

The days away passed as an aching joy, eerily similar to the weekend in Santa Fe a year earlier—memories stillborn.

Pain puts us all on the run for relief . . . to the refrigerator, the medicine cabinet, the bottle, the mall—the list is long. I responded to the cancer pain by shooting up at the golf course.

When my mind could not ponder any more cancer, I thought about golf. I subscribed to a golf magazine, I read golf books, I bought golf equipment, I watched Jack Nicklaus golf videos, I practiced golf in the backyard with little plastic golf balls. I came close to overdosing on golf. Racinda didn't say much about it, at least most of the time.

Late one afternoon after work, about the time concrete dinner plans are set, I announced I was heading out to "hit a few balls."

"Oh, do you *have* to do that tonight? I wanted to eat together—haven't you had enough golf this week?" Racinda said, in less than sweet fashion. In fact, her acidic accusation stoked me real good. We were both ready for some "garbage time."

"Golleeee, can't I get any breaks? I work like a dog all day long, and now I just want to relax a little—to get away from what I'm dealing with around here, and this is what I get?" I said with huff and puff. In my own defense, I was resorting to this snarly bombast less than in the past, but emoting anger is like riding a bike—you just never forget how.

Racinda shot a pained look and left for our upstairs bedroom. As usual, her retreat angered me more than if she had clanked me with a pot—I just couldn't stand being unable to explain precisely how she was making me feel.

But instead of following her, slinging more trash on the way, I let her go. I was in the mood to stir up some self-pity, and it seems easier to mix a batch of that on your own.

I rumbled and mumbled around the garage, collecting my golf stuff, slamming my clubs into the car trunk. I was about to grab my keys and exit the driveway with flying gravel when Racinda approached me in our mudroom. *Ah, this is good! I could almost hear my mind purr. I have a few choice words to dump on this woman.*

"Honey, I am really sorry for what I said," Racinda said with sincerity. I detected not a hint of seething sarcasm.

Huh? I thought.

"You are absolutely right—you do deserve a break. I want you to go play golf and enjoy yourself."

Now wait a minute! What's going on here?

"If you are not home in time for dinner, I'll save a plate you can heat up." With that she smiled and walked away.

Now what was I to do? Here I am, filled to the brim with self-righteous bile, and she's not playing by the rules! She's supposed to give me a reason to deposit this stuff on her, but she ruined it all by being so nice! What's the catch?

Convinced I had missed something, my mind a mental train wreck, I stomped in pursuit, finding her walking briskly on the treadmill, *humming*. She *smiled* at me. This was terrible!

Hoping to rediscover the old Racinda hiding in this

impostor, I let her have a few choice comments, some of those I had been practicing during my self-pity monologue. She just kept walking, smiled while looking at me, and said: "I told you I was wrong. I made a mistake. I'm sorry."

What do you say in response to that? Shaking my head, I left her on the treadmill. Now she had me thinking about how I had ripped into her. I was starting to feel guilty about how I had acted. *I couldn't play golf now! I needed to buttress my reputation in the family—wasn't it about time for dinner?*

Later, after my anger and confusion dissipated, I told Racinda I was sorry for how I had acted—and would she tell me just exactly what was going on? "This is different," I said, in awe and with some fear.

So we talked for a long time, a very adult conversation, two equals seeking to understand and be understood. This felt nice. *I kind of like this.* And sure enough, it was that Incredible Lady who had her miracle-working hands in this, not just teaching Racinda about needing to admit sin, and to stop seeking to control other people, and how to rightly stand up for herself—but indirectly teaching me, too.

If only the Incredible Lady were a golf instructor.

Early the next week Racinda went to the hospital to have a catheter implanted for the first round of the Texas Ranger's chemo regimen. We were not at ease with unfolding events, but the aggressiveness of the doctor was comforting. We did have one card left to play—a final consultation with a third oncologist. It was Racinda's wish to have three opinions before any drugs entered her body.

We wanted to have the third doctor visit before the port was installed in her chest, but the timing was off. So again Racinda was prepped for the minor surgery and wheeled into the familiar operating chambers.

She came out less than an hour later and within minutes felt ready to exit the hospital and drive to meet the new oncologist. But the surgeon would not release her. So we waited—15, 30, 45 minutes.

Cancer makes you jumpy, so when any medical test or procedure does not go as planned, the questions fly in your head like hungry bats: *Why is this taking so long? Did they see something else in there when they were poking around? Was it a tumor the size of a potato? Why aren't they telling us something?*

After an hour passed the doctor returned and said it was possible that Racinda's lung had been pierced accidentally during the catheter installation. Her lung would need to be X-rayed in several hours.

Seriously, you have thoughts like this: *What a relief—no more cancer, just maybe a punctured lung!*

Racinda dressed hurriedly and we fled the hospital— scarcely enough time now to make the appointment with doctor number three. As we raced along the highway, Racinda grew uncomfortable, squirming to ease the pressure and pain in her chest. If not for her raw determination to get more answers on her disease, we would have turned back to the hospital.

The doctor had a small suite in an office building across the street from a hospital. I noted on the door that his specialty was "breast diseases." Was it possible that someone who concentrated on breasts had a treatment up his sleeve that could avoid nearly killing Racinda? The hope, only 15 watts bright, still burned. I filled out forms as Racinda gave me verbal instructions. Even talking shot pain down her side.

The receptionist was so cheerful I became suspicious—*What's the game they are playing here?* I'd not seen such a weightless spirit in other cancer shops. In the examining room I helped Racinda don her gown, cloth instead of paper—nice touch.

The doctor arrived, a lean man of angular features and coal-black hair, wearing cowboy boots, a western shirt with pearl button snaps, and a string tie. He looked like the sheriff of an 1800s cow town, a movie-star-stud guy.

This oncologist was nice but all business. He asked many questions and fully reviewed the case. He wanted to know treatment plans recommended by the other doctors. He knew of the national reputation of our Texas Ranger doctor. He seemed to know his stuff.

As we flipped question after question his way, he quickly and convincingly answered each one, like a gunfighter drawing his sidearm and blasting tin cans thrown in the sky. I warmed to his straight-shooting ways. He maintained his

M.D. diplomacy when responding to the plans of the other docs, but he stated his opinions clearly, like the jab of a sharp spur.

He agreed with the aggressive approaches, although he implied the Texas Ranger was proposing more ammo than necessary. His plan would involve a run of chemotherapy, a drug called Taxotere, which he said bluntly, "is the best drug we have to fight breast cancer." And then he wanted the bone marrow transplant, too, at an in-patient hospital program.

Our time ended and he made no mealymouthed appeal for our business. He knew that we knew that he was man enough for the job. In my mind he became *the Sheriff*. He closed with a sturdy handshake, wished us luck, flashed that white-teeth, lean-jawed smile, and hurried out. I thought I heard the whinny of a horse tied out back to a hitching post.

We started back to the hospital, caught in the molasses of after-work traffic. Her chest aching, Racinda was in no mood for a debriefing and reclined the seat, shutting her eyes.

It was a good thing she couldn't converse, because I might have unloaded my opinions with the finesse of a double blow from a two-barrel shotgun. I liked this doc! In fact, I was ecstatic. This was the gunslinger I wanted to face down the mean, bad cancer dudes hanging out in our town. He was gentle and caring, but I sensed would be cold and ruthless when required. I could see him striding down Main Street, pinching red cheeks of little children while tipping his hat and saying "Mornin,' ma'am" to their mothers. Then out of the corner of his eye, spotting some dirty Bart cancer *hombre* pulling his gun, the sheriff would spin, draw both six-shooters, and plug the miserable vermin dead.

But what did Racinda think?

As we snailed along, I listed in my mind the pros and cons of all three cancer-fighting doctors. The Sheriff rose to the top of my list. He seemed to have the blend of skill, courage, and style we were looking for. The choice seemed obvious, but I bit my tongue and kept my yap shut.

We arrived back at the hospital at 6:30 P.M. The X ray confirmed the doctor's hunch; Racinda had a pneumothorax, caused by air leaking from her lung, and was sent immediately into the hospital. A small tube was surgically inserted into her chest cavity to release pressure, and with heavy medication, she finally escaped the pain and slept.

The next day Racinda came home and the decision-making process intensified. We delayed the Texas doctor's chemotherapy and heard the BMT orientation at a local hospital. We didn't talk much about the Sheriff, although Racinda admitted she liked him.

During the week I called the Texas clinic and spoke to an insurance expert in the accounting department. I explained our situation and gave him the name of the insurance company. He acknowledged that this company was not eager to pay for high-dose chemo/BMT.

"Well, what do you do if the insurance company doesn't pay?" I stammered.

He paused and said, "We've never attempted to collect from the patient." So the hearts were big in Texas, too.

We had to decide. With more than two weeks gone since removal of the cancerous lumps, Racinda wanted to turn the cancer-fighting cavalry loose in her bloodstream. A fourth cancer doctor was found for a bonus consultation. This man was not a specialist in breast cancer, but he was respected by one of Racinda's friends. Since he would not treat Racinda, he should truly be an unbiased party.

After reviewing the options this oncologist said magic words, ones Racinda had prayed secretly to hear. He spoke kindly and diplomatically about the other doctors, then in quiet tones said, "I certainly would send my wife to [the Sheriff] if she had breast cancer."

And that was it. Decision made. Chemotherapy started two days later at the Sheriff's office.

Get outta Dodge!

12

The BMT

June 1998

NOW THAT WE HAD A DOCTOR, the next step was to learn more about the terrifying bone marrow transplant procedure. An appointment was scheduled at the center where the Sheriff referred his patients.

This city hospital was large—the parking garage crammed, the halls full of patients, visitors, and hospital personnel moving at a slow-run pace.

The three of us—Noelle had a day off and came along—found the BMT unit on the fourth floor. Facing us were two wide doors plastered with warnings, since BMT patients must be scrupulously protected from the risk of infection. We entered through the first barrier, a small room separated by two more doors from the BMT area. In this anteroom, an air-locked space that prevents contaminated air from entering the unit, we each slipped on a long yellow hospital gown and covered our feet with booties. Our bags and purses were covered in plastic.

Looking like Three-Stooge surgeons, we entered the BMT unit and walked down a highly waxed hallway to a nurse's station. We were taken to an empty patient room. The heavy wood door, which had a small window, clicked shut behind us. The room was equipped with multiple gadgets and monitors near bedside. There was a well-stocked workstation for the nurses and a private bathroom.

The afternoon passed as a progression of doctors and others discussed Racinda's case and the proposed treatment. I took notes but soon lost my ability to concentrate; the process described was long, complicated, and devastating.

Before entering the hospital Racinda would donate her own stem cells, the young, fast-growing blood cells born, like all cells, in the bone marrow. These stem cells would be frozen until she was ready to receive them back via transfusion after the high-dose chemotherapy. The stem cells would enter her body to jump-start her recovery and begin the delicate rebuilding of her decimated immune system. Without this stem cell rescue effort, her recovery would take a long time—if she ever made it back at all. Even if the process went well, she would live with a compromised immune system for up to two weeks before the danger passed.

The entire stay would last about twenty-one days, and Racinda would not leave her room until almost the time to exit the hospital. After discharge she would have to stay within minutes of the hospital, until her blood recovered enough ability to fight infection so that she could live at home safely.

I looked at Racinda. Her skin was rosy and clear. She exercised almost daily, ate abundant fruit and vegetables, and was at her optimum weight. Her curly hair was shiny black. She appeared younger than forty-six, and I couldn't remember when she had looked so healthy. Yet, voluntarily we were going to pump chemicals into her body that would essentially execute her immune system and possibly take her life. What was wrong with this picture? No wonder I had trouble listening attentively to the doctors. And just what might this high-powered, extended medical expedition cost?

After receiving the overview of the treatment plan—certainly in the nick of time—a psychologist came in to evaluate (perhaps resuscitate?) our withered emotions. She asked questions about the feelings-side of facing Racinda's illness and the proposed treatment. Since post-hospital care would influence the speed and success of Racinda's recovery, she wanted to know who would be her go-to caregiver. Of course that would be me.

We explained that our sources of strength were our faith and family, a response met with the supportive "hmmmm" and nod that must be taught in all learning halls of psychology.

We met last with one of the unit's chief doctors, a tall man of boisterous confidence and golden credentials. After hearing his thoughts I knew the time was right to pop the sensitive insurance coverage question. His answer had a familiar ring—

insurance companies often fought BMT treatment plans, but the hospital would mount the campaign with the insurer. We should stay out of it. That was fine with me.

The hospital would allow two months to obtain insurance approval, so in the meantime, Racinda needed to proceed with her "warm-up" chemotherapy treatments.

Every three weeks we went to the Sheriff's office for blood testing followed by the drip-drip-drip of the cancer poison. This chemo chamber was more intimate than the one experienced a year earlier. The room had just a few stuffed chairs, as normally only one or two other patients were on hand—women often wearing scarves or hats, compatriots on the cancer battlefield.

Conversation sparked the sharing of war stories. I felt I was in the company of personified courage as each woman related, many times with a wry smile, tales of often multiple engagements with the enemy. It reminded me of army nights when battle-worn lifers reminisced over their beers of tragic and comic moments in a soldier's life, all told with a sad fondness.

About halfway through Racinda's chemo bottle, I would slip out for sub sandwiches so we could eat while the fluid dripped into her arm. After several hours the bottle emptied, and we left hurriedly, glad another treatment could be crossed from the list. More weary than before, Racinda rested for a day or two. Again the anti-nausea medicine worked; she never got sick.

The BMT

With decisions made and treatment under way, we settled into our summer routine, awaiting our fate with the insurance company. Early in the process we'd learned that since Racinda was a public school teacher, her coverage was through a self-funded company. The insurer with hostility toward BMT was just the claims administrator. This was good news, but we still faithfully said our prayers as the weeks passed. Although Racinda wavered some, wondering still if such radical treatment was wise, her resolve to proceed hardened like concrete poured on a hot summer day. But we just had to have insurance coverage.

In spite of hope inspired by a new shampoo, Racinda's hair thinned. First the old hats, then the hated wig reappeared. Some mornings the water drained slowly from the shower, the flow dammed by the clump of black hair clogging the drain.

I hated the hats, reminders of bad days I thought we'd not see again. So we shopped for designer baseball caps at a department store. Racinda tried them on furtively—not wanting other shoppers to catch a peek of her balding scalp. She found one we both liked, and now she had a new-hat look for her second encounter with chemotherapy.

Through unusual circumstances I had acquired the tail end of a golf membership at a local club, and to make my investment pay, I calculated that I needed to play 250 holes in six weeks.

I hadn't played for thirty years, and I had the game to show it. Now I played almost every day. And the more I played and the harder I tried to correct my flaws—the worse things got. I was no longer an amiable social golfer; I'd become a "golf-aholic"—"Just *one* more hole and I'll quit." Yeah, right! It wasn't until the golf nearly killed me that I knew how low in my addiction I'd sunk.

At twilight on a stormy July evening, with lightning flashing from huge thunderheads, instead of calling it quits I decided to play just a few more holes, a poor decision that took me farther away from the clubhouse. After hitting several nice fairway wood and long iron shots, deeds that left me gripped in golf euphoria, I almost forgot the encircling storm. I approached a hole with a small pond on the right. The water hazard was not a factor; from my ball location, I had an open, land route to the pin. I could have rolled the ball home with my putter. But then the troll who lives in my golf bag awakened, whispering to my subconscious: *Bruce! See that water? Why don't you hit the ball over there?*

I selected a wedge, and defying laws of physics and perhaps even gravity, I slammed the ball on a perfect 30-degree line to the right, directly into the pond. The ball splashed, the green scum parting and closing as though welcoming a long-lost son.

The storm was closer now, but rather than just giving up and moving quickly to the clubhouse, I muttered dark words and dug through the reeds around the pond for misplaced balls of other golfers. I found three, and seeking to regain confidence, I dropped the balls in front of the pond and took aim for the green on the other side. Resolutely I hammered all of them into the water—plunk . . . plunk . . . plunk.

Desperate now, my self-esteem in meltdown, as the thunder boomed I dug a range ball from my bag and with a mini-miracle chopped it over the water. I walked triumphantly to the ball, but with the howling wind and angry clouds urging me to seek shelter, as a final sign of my victory over the contrary wedge and *the pond*, I turned and took aim to hit the range ball back over the water. The troll giggled, I swung mightily, the ball barreled on a low line into the pond.

Not sure I was still sane, I hurried through the gusting wind and scattered raindrops to the next tee box. The lightning strikes were close enough to make me not want to stand on the elevated tee, but deranged by golf fever, I plopped a ball on the fairway and raised an iron above my head. Lightning struck close, so I picked up the ball, abandoned my clubs, and ran in a crouch to a low spot by a wall of timbers at the course's boundary. With the storm booming and cracking on all sides, I lay on my back, wedged against the wooden barrier.

The storm's cool air was making me shiver, so when a break came in the lightning barrage, I sprinted to the pull cart for my jacket. As I pulled on the coat, a man on a powered golf cart motored up. I thought this must be a course marshal or a good Samaritan golfer stopping to rescue me. The man called out through the splatter of rain, "You better be careful. The lightning is close." *This is true*, I thought. And when I expected him to say next, "Hey, do you want a ride to the clubhouse?" he yelled instead, "Say, did you see a black towel? I lost it up here somewhere."

I shook my head and he sped away into the storm, retracing his route back toward the previous hole. If this was an insane asylum, I knew now I wasn't the only inmate.

With the clouds rolling low and electricity crackling in the air, I again had to find cover. I took several steps toward my makeshift bunker and then a huge "boom-crack" shook the hillside. My adrenaline surging, I ran three steps, then leaped and rolled on the ground against the timbers, like a marine grunt reacting to a mortar round. Plastered against the earth, wondering if I might soon give my life for a very bad round of golf, I heard a voice say tentatively from somewhere behind the timbers, "Do you want to come inside for a while?"

A kind homeowner had seen the lightning flash followed by my flying leap—"Golly, Martha! I think I just saw a golfer get killed!"—which looked like a man receiving a direct hit. I accepted the offer, scampering like a refugee across a border to freedom. My host and his wife were watching a TV movie, so I joined their viewing as the storm wailed on, they in their pajamas and robes, I in my grass-stained shorts and soaked shirt. We had a lovely chat, and after a half hour the man gave me a ride to the clubhouse.

I arrived home after dark and explained my adventure to a worried Racinda, who had seen the dark clouds over the golf course. After assuring her I was sound of body, I slipped furtively to the garage. With the rain still pounding the roof, I dropped a rubber mat on the floor, threw down some wiffle golf balls, and tried several swings. I knew I would not sleep until I had a new cure for my horrible, very bad, suicidal, water-seeking slice.

∼

I had not heard the word *pheresis* before breast cancer expanded my vocabulary. *Pheresis* is actually one of the nice words in the cancer dictionary, because it describes a nearly painless step in some types of the BMT process.

On a warm Monday morning in mid-August, we reported to the hospital's pheresis unit. This was the launch of the BMT journey—treatments and recovery that would last for months. The hurdles were behind us. First the long-awaited letter had arrived from the insurance company; Racinda's treatment had been approved without contest. Next several tests were done to make sure Racinda's body could take the barrage of high-dose chemotherapy. Everything looked good. Finally, a Hickman catheter was implanted just below her collarbone in a large vein leading to her heart. Except for occasional doubts, Racinda was determined to face the uncertainties of the days ahead.

Pheresis involves taking the blood from your body and sending it through a cell separator machine that removes the stem cells before giving the blood back. Since Racinda had the catheter with two ports, out and in hoses were connected and she sat back to work on her cross-stitch as the machine hissed, whirled, and hummed. A small plastic bag collected the precious stem cells, which later would go to a freezer for safekeeping.

I stayed beside Racinda for a while. The morning news babbled from a distant TV, and my attention swayed to the drama unfolding in the next cubicle. A man about my age was immobilized with the in and out needles/tubes in both arms. We learned that he was a donor, giving up his stem cells for a younger brother recently diagnosed with leukemia. Since the donor had no need for a chemotherapy catheter, he had to come for three or four days, have an IV needle planted in both arms, then sit quietly for five or more hours. Literally, the man was preparing a gift of life for his brother. This example of unsung, courageous sacrifice is seen daily along the cancer front.

I left to do some work, returning later to share lunch. By early afternoon, all of Racinda's blood had circled once through the exotic machine and what looked like less than a pint of stem cells was collected in the bag. The nurses pronounced this a successful harvest, and after giving her a shot of medication to stimulate the bone marrow to overproduce stem cells, we left for the day.

Noelle needed to return to college for the fall semester, so we picked up Racinda on her last day at the pheresis unit and left immediately for Chicago. We returned Monday night and on Tuesday packed Racinda's clothes and other belongings for her hospital stay. Since the threat of infection would be one of her enemies after the chemotherapy bombed out her immune system, all of her clothes had to be new or washed and there were strict limits on what personal items could be brought to her hospital room. I've never found packing to be such a joyless experience. Everything about this experience was strange and ominous.

That night a pastor and friends came from our church to offer encouragement and prayer. After our guests left, Racinda and I went to bed. I held her close, not knowing how long it might be—if ever—I would do such a normal, yet treasured act as lying next to the person I loved. But this night, my body freshened by the sweet tears of prayer, I drifted swiftly to a sleep, long and deep.

The next morning we loaded our van with plastic bags of Racinda's belongings, as well as suitcases containing my clothes and work projects.

We arrived at the hospital, and after check-in, took the elevator to the BMT unit. In Racinda's room nurses checked her vital signs and drew blood samples. In the meantime I hauled the baggage to the unit, each time gowning up and down as I passed through the airlock chamber. Before bringing Racinda's books, CD player, and pictures to the room, I wiped everything with disinfectant.

Around noon we could leave for Racinda's last lunch, at a

favorite Chinese restaurant. There in the noisy, laughing mid-day crowd we ate quietly, trying gamely to manufacture normal conversation and happy feelings.

Back at the hospital Racinda slipped on her gown and prepared for combat.

Since the catheter in her chest would be used for infusion of the chemotherapy drugs and fluids, another catheter had to go in her arm for blood draws. Again I had to watch a nurse work for a long while to plant the tube in one of Racinda's delicate blood vessels. And, as usual, I ached when the needle made her wince.

The hours passed slowly as nurses and doctors came and left. To fortify her body, three units of blood were administered. After dinner Racinda reminded me that once chemotherapy began, she would be sedated and might not be coherent. After weeks of preparing herself for this journey to the townships bordering death, she had several requests. One of them angered me. She asked that if during the treatment she was troubled by a bad dream or was otherwise distressed, I should repeat to her a favorite Scripture-based phrase. This was a plan Racinda and her counselor, the Incredible Lady, had devised. The phrase I was to say was, "Nothing is impossible with God."

Why this bothered me I'm not sure; I certainly was willing for God to do the impossible. But as sometimes happens, here at the moment when I wanted to say the most affectionate and supportive words, I had a chunk of resentment stuck in my throat. Neither of us had the energy or chutzpah to wage an argument in the BMT unit, but our parting was tense.

I drove to a nearby condominium where some friends had arranged for me to stay. This was the first of many strange, lonely nights. In good health I was able to leave Racinda in her quiet, isolated, otherworldly room. But though my normal-looking body walked the streets, sat in restaurants, and consumed coffee over the morning paper, I didn't really escape the hospital room where details of my future were being shaped. The things that normally satisfied and brought joy tasted flat. That's just the nature of the connection to someone who's hurting. Try as you might, you can't control the color and altitude of your moods.

The high-dose chemotherapy began on Thursday. The clear poison arrived in a glass bottle so large it resembled a two-liter Coke bottle bulked up with steroids.

Before hanging the bottle and attaching the line to Racinda's catheter, the nurse donned a protective gown and slipped on thick rubber gloves. Apparently this juice was as potent as battery acid. To help protect Racinda's major organs during the chemotherapy, she received quarts of benign fluids dripped in via IV. Several monitors measured this procedure. With annoying regularity bags emptied or filled and alarm buzzers rang.

In the initial stages Racinda was awake and passed the

time listening to music, reading, and playing solitaire. But by about noon on Friday the anti-nausea medication hit in force and she fell asleep, not to awaken in any meaningful way for three days. This was a mercy. During those long hours of non-stop chemo treatment, she drifted in and out of awareness. Sometimes she would lift through her haze and converse lucidly. Other times her comments were goofy, the same kind of twilight-zone interactions you have with a sleepwalker. When the ordeal ended, she didn't remember a thing.

I sat by her bed, watching the chemo bottles slowly drip, keeping an eye on the video screen that showed her heart rate and blood pressure. At times I stirred enough energy to tap out work on my computer, and several times a day I plugged in the modem to collect e-mail. The buzzers on the machines beeped, and if the nurse didn't arrive promptly, Racinda would rouse and say, "Turn that thing off!"

The nurses worked twelve-hour shifts, flitting frequently in and out of the room. The doctors came twice a day, wrapped like me in surgical gowns. The care was excellent.

While Racinda slept I watched. The hours dragged, time marked by the fading of outside light as the sun passed over the hospital, then made its evening exit behind the mountains. When the walls closed in and were about to crush the breath from me, I stood quietly and tiptoed for the door. Almost without fail—her eyes tightly shut—Racinda would say, "Honey, where are you going?" I would explain, and she would say weakly, "Okay. But don't be gone too long . . . " She would retreat into her haze, as quickly as a cuckoo vanishing behind the door of its clock.

I stayed away as long as I could. There was not much to do in the room, and watching her hour after hour, my hope fell. I knew the chemotherapy was spreading through her body, waves of liquid death, much like napalm dropped on a village, destroying everything, the good cells dying with the bad. And until the chemo stopped, her condition would get worse before it could possibly get better.

By Saturday noon I couldn't take much more. Racinda's sister was to arrive hours later that afternoon, but with Racinda so out of sync with reality, she didn't compute that I was leaving earlier than necessary for the airport. I used my break from the BMT to inject some courage into a wavering heart.

I met Roberta at the gate and we drove to the hospital. In between naps, Racinda was glad to have her sister nearby. She welcomed the company but more than anything was glad for me—now I could take more breaks and might even accomplish some work. Later Allan arrived to drive his aunt home for the evening.

The next morning Roberta returned. After visiting with the doctor during the morning rounds and eating lunch, I left Roberta in charge and dashed home. With each familiar sight and odor, a mini-celebration erupted in my soul. I sat on the deck and rubbed Nala's stomach, relishing her slobber on my hand. Even the mail pile was intriguing, and the few minutes of watching TV and chatting with Allan were a treasure. How I missed our normal life, the sublime blessing of eating, sleeping, working, and playing in the place called home.

Soon the buzzer sounded in the dryer and after packing up my clean clothes and playing just one game of pool with Allan, I said good-bye and drove the sixty miles to the hospital. I reentered Racinda's room with a bounce in my step, my outlook refreshed.

With Racinda in her final day of high-dose chemotherapy, we counted the hours until the last bottle would drain dry. The doctors assured us the treatment was proceeding without a hitch, and Racinda's mood was bright. Before Roberta left each evening, she and I stood on opposite sides of the bed, holding hands with Racinda, and said our prayers of gratitude and request. And how Roberta prayed, a battle-tested spiritual warrior, confidently informing the Commander in Chief of our need for re-supply of His healing power. This soft-voiced, gentle woman, pumped up with holy power, was ready and able to call for God's finest weapons in the assault against her sister's disease. My prayers were more like an accountant calmly sharing last quarter's numbers with the CEO. Techniques differ, but God is a great listener.

And to all prayers, with her eyes closed, Racinda nodded her head and through dry, parted lips whispered, "Yes."

The BMT

Our D-Day—"done with chemo"—arrived, and Roberta and I took our assigned seats by Racinda's bed. The last bag of medicine was attached, and we watched as the fluid slowly dribbled through the line. With the final drip the buzzer sounded and the nurse came and turned off the chemo spigot. We celebrated with subdued cheers. This was ground zero, death valley, the bottom of the pit. Unknown, difficult days were ahead, but the artillery in the chemical battle fell silent for good.

In the hours that followed, one after another IV lines and catheters were unhooked and by evening Racinda sat up on the edge of the bed. With a nurse on each side, she stood and took several wobbly steps. As she shuffled along, stooped over, her body quivering, I saw not a wife's vibrant frame but the dried shell of an ancient woman.

Details of the following days have eroded, leaving just unforgettable impressions, jutting like limestone towers from the base of memories. When alone with her, while she slept I gazed at the familiar face, skin tightened and off-white, her delicately sculpted skull adorned with scattered strands of lifeless hair. Was this a snapshot from a time to come when aging lovers come to the stop where one lies to rest and the other walks on alone? Before me like a preview, I saw the death of Racinda's flesh.

But this foreboding was overshadowed by a brighter

insight of love. In some recess of my heart a light flickered, and I saw that the Racinda I loved was more than the condition of her bones, blood, and tissue. I loved *her*—the eternal intangible spirit and essence. And with a new vision of love I grew more afraid that this calamity would steal the fragile body in which my loved one lived.

Hoping to blunt the numbing side effect of one chemotherapy drug, I rubbed lotion on her calves and feet. Weak and worn, Racinda could only whisper her appreciation. She had no strength in her lifeless flesh to muster any words or caresses to feed my pleasure. But as I massaged her toes, flames of desire spread in my body, crackling and spitting like a fire loose in dry underbrush. I was bewildered by such sensations, but an unexpected satisfaction claimed me.

I knew now, as I touched the cool, dry, and brittle skin, that my love for her was anchored in solid stuff. Winds might howl and assail this fortress called us, but we would survive.

13

Danger Zone

September 1998

THE HIGH-DOSE CHEMOTHERAPY barrage was over, but now other dangers threatened Racinda's health.

The medical staff warned that she would soon be "neutropenic," a five-dollar word meaning "wiped out"—the time when depleted blood cell counts would essentially leave her without an immune system. Her body's bone marrow, the efficient cell factory where red and white cells and platelets are manufactured, had been annihilated. Until the transplant of her stem cells and their hoped-for success in booting-up her anti-disease defense system, she had no resources to conquer even the wimpiest infection. Germs, not breast cancer, were the immediate enemies.

Sanitation security tightened. No flowers or plants, which host bacteria, were allowed. Racinda could drink only purified water. Visitors with symptoms of illness were barred. I washed my hands with hypoallergenic soap and hot water, and before handing Racinda even a glass of water, I faithfully slipped on the latex gloves.

Still regrouping from the chemotherapy and neutropenia, Racinda slept lightly. Not wanting to disturb her, Roberta and I huddled at the end of the bed to whisper conversations. Eyes closed and breathing deeply, Racinda seemed oblivious, until our chat took an intriguing track—then she'd join in. Once she interjected, from out of apparent sound sleep, "Could we talk about something more positive, please?"

When awake Racinda felt too lousy to laugh; I teased her anyway. Flat on her back receiving a blood transfusion from one IV line and medicine from another, I'd say: "I suppose you're not going to want to go dancing again tonight?" And with not enough energy to speak a comeback, she would shoot me a look girls use in fourth grade, the disgusted, hands-on-hips expression that says *I'm-not-going-to-honor-a-subhuman-slug-like-you-with-even-a-word.* Then in the most endearing way she'd finish me off by rolling her eyes. I laughed with joy every time this happened, aware that I was seeing a replay from childhood, the little girl I hadn't known.

Not one to sit around after chemotherapy ended, Racinda asked that her physical therapy begin. One of the anti-cancer drugs had stunned nerve endings throughout her body, especially in her hands and feet. And the chemical warfare had left her legs wobbly. The therapist demonstrated exercises and showed her how to navigate with a walker. He also encouraged me to help Racinda practice walking by making several spins with her around the room each day.

I pulled her upright and stood at her side, one arm wrapped tightly around her waist, our free hands clasped (mine in latex glove) to the front. Like a tipsy couple taking the dance floor at a country western bar, we gingerly slid forward with tiny steps. Without warning Racinda's legs gave way, and she swayed and dipped toward the floor. I caught her on the way down, hauled her up, and off we glided again, giggles and all. Even without music, before long we had that BMT two-step down cold.

Just one short round trip and Racinda would collapse into her chair or the bed. Exhausted by just a few steps, she needed sleep. As I watched the sunken body, her breath coming in shallow wheezes, a fear flitted into my thoughts: *My wife looks like she's seventy years old. What if she never recovers? What will our life be like?*

Each night as dusk fell, Racinda asked the nurse for the evening medicine that aided her sleep. I leaned over her to say our goodnight prayer and with a washed, but ungloved hand, rubbed her cheek and kissed her forehead with unsterilized lips.

Then I left her disinfected solitary confinement, the music playing softly and the bedside paraphernalia clicking and whirring. The two worlds seemed not of the same planet—the controlled hospital indoors reeking of antiseptic and chemicals, and the chaotic outdoors, pungent with odors of bus exhaust, dirt, fading flowers, and grass. How thankful I was for the pleasure of inhaling the night air. And how I longed for the time when she, too, would draw again a full gasp of such a fragrant summer evening.

There I stood on the first tee, waggling my club, wiggling my behind, wondering what orbit my ball would soon enter. I felt some guilt that I was puttering around on a golf course while Racinda was stuck in a hospital room.

A friend who knew I needed a break from the cancer ordeal had suggested a nine-hole therapy. So with Roberta on duty at bedside, and after Racinda's blessing, I had slipped out for some R and R.

I appreciated my friend's forceful insertion into my BMT vigil; I was feeling lonely but hesitant to admit it—how could I indulge self-pity when I wasn't the one fighting sickness?

I had learned that when cancer comes knocking, some friends and acquaintances stay close—others drift away. My theory is that cancer scares the bejeebers out of everybody, but since the disease is so widespread, most people have acquired basic skills in relating to the "doomed one" during an initial occurrence. Flowers and cards are brought on several visits during diagnosis, treatment, and recovery. Then everyone breathes a collective sigh of relief as post-chemo hair sprouts and "normal" life resumes.

But if the cancer comes back, what was manageable fear the first time for outsiders becomes throat-tightening terror.

Doesn't this mean she'll die?—you can almost hear the thoughts of some people clanking like dry gears. Not knowing what to say, or worried that some unintended comment will be devastating, many people take the safe option and just stay away.

I know . . . I've done the same thing.

The truth is, you don't need speeches to comfort the hurting. I'd seen this years earlier when my mother died. The day before the funeral, some of my father's fishing and hunting buddies, his brothers in the Lord, stopped at the house. They weren't a polished bunch. They said little but surrounded my sad daddy, wrapping beefy arms and bear-paw hands around his shoulders and neck, trying to hug away his hurt. Then wiping their eyes on shirtsleeves, they left. A squad of angels wearing dress blues could not have brought comfort any better.

My golfing buddy asked me how Racinda was doing and how I was doing. A cancer survivor himself, he knew I needed someone to help carry the load for a few hours.

If only the game of golf had such empathy. No mysterious grace descended to make the crooked go straight. I hacked, chopped, and sliced in ways more creative and heinous than before. But I returned to the hospital refreshed, my spirits revived by an afternoon spent on the grass and in the trees—lots of trees.

≈

With the "excitement" of high-dose chemotherapy over, the waiting game made the hours drag. No one could predict the length of the hospital stay, but the best-case guess was about two more weeks.

Each day I arrived in the robing room before 9:00 A.M. with newspaper and coffee cup in hand. I knew exactly which type gown was most comfy, and I could now easily stretch what seemed like size 8 booties over my size 10 sneakers.

Racinda was recharged and fresh after sleep, bath, and breakfast. She always gave me the smile and "Hi, honthey!" said with a novocaine-like lisp because the nerve endings around her mouth also were numb temporarily. While setting up my laptop computer, I got the scoop on the quality of last night's sleep and performance of the nursing crew.

After each meal Racinda's teeth and mouth had to be cleaned with an oral rinse applied with a sponge brush. Since her platelet count was low and still falling, any bleeding was avoided, including a cut on her gums with a standard toothbrush. The mouth care was important because mouth sores often were another chemotherapy side effect, so severe that eating was nearly impossible.

The medical staff made their rounds by mid-morning. Usually they came in a pack of eight or so, doctors, residents, physician's assistants, psychologist, nurses, and others with roles not always clear to me. Racinda was carefully examined and questioned. Sometimes I would chime in with an observation. The consensus was that Racinda had weathered the chemotherapy well, but now the impact of the drugs would be seen in dangerously low blood cell counts.

Roberta would arrive and relieve me while I slipped away to work for a few hours. She took over mouth care, rubbing Racinda's legs and feet, and helping Racinda keep her lungs free of fluid by having her blow into a tube attached to a plastic apparatus.

One afternoon I broke the routine by attending a family support group meeting in the BMT unit. Two of us joined the staff psychologist—the other family member older, the father of a young man only recently diagnosed with leukemia.

We sat around a small table, nipping at our juice and cookies, trying to assign words to elusive feelings. Conversation was constipated. Chitchat on sports and the weather comes hard when loved ones are flirting with death behind the closed doors just across the hall. We did share enough of our stories, though, to make occasional encounters in the robing room thereafter more meaningful.

Because all of the patients were kept in sanitary confinement, I never saw the man's son. So I had to imagine a face while saying prayers for him. One afternoon I encountered the boy's mother in a hospital hallway. When I asked how her son was doing, she answered painfully, her eyes glazed, "We almost lost him." I never heard the final outcome.

The days clicked by—watching the clock, waiting for the doctor's insights, receiving more blood, checking of vital signs, exercising per instruction of the physical therapist, learning the results of the daily blood tests, and hoping that no infection would come calling.

Meals were bland but something to anticipate. Many undergoing this treatment don't have much appetite and need to be sustained intravenously. But Racinda's strong will served her well as she forced down as much food as she could.

After one solid lunch I urged her to use her lung-expanding toy. She was puffing heartily as I cheered her on but overdid it. In an instant the meal was back with us. With so little strength anyway, the vomiting left Racinda spent. She collapsed on her pillow and wearily closed her eyes. Another detour on the recovery trail.

That was the last time that day I asked her to blow into the little tube.

Although Racinda remained depleted and vulnerable, she was doing as well as could be expected and not in immediate danger. After our daytime shift at the BMT ended, I could leave and not worry about setbacks overnight. On one night much like the others, I left the hospital mid-evening and enjoyed the short walk back to my lodging, a basement suite provided by gracious friends. After watching TV, I read before falling asleep.

Deep in the night the phone rang. I jumped awake, my heart pounding. Since this wasn't my home, normally I didn't answer the phone. After several rings someone else picked up. I put my head back on the pillow, hoping the call wasn't for me—it would be the hospital. There were a few moments of silence, then from two floors above, I heard footsteps, the muffled tap-tap of bare feet on carpet, coming closer and closer. Dread surged through me like a flood. My door creaked open and in the half-light I saw a portable phone in my host's hand.

"It's your wife," he said.

Warily I took the phone. *What in heaven's name was happening?* A nurse was on the line and said that Racinda wanted to talk to me. This was totally weird. She came on and lisped a few words. Then her voice faded away and the phone clicked dead.

My imagination raced. *Had she somehow climbed out of bed and hurt herself? She sounded borderline delirious.* I calmed my thoughts and dialed her room—someone should be nearby. The same nurse answered and apologized for how I'd been cut off. She told me that two of Racinda's medications had combined disastrously to severely reduce her blood pressure. An alert staff had caught the problem early and reversed the downward trend, but there had been concern enough to summon the night-duty resident. When the situation stabilized, a frightened Racinda wanted me called.

"Everything is fine now," the nurse said cheerily.

After hanging up I sat dazed on my bed. Going back to sleep was appealing, but I remembered other stops on this journey where very bad news had come in the wake of chipper statements like "Everything is fine now."

I dressed and slipped out of the house. It was after 2:00 A.M. and the streets were quiet. As I walked toward the hospital, my mind trembled: *After enduring the horrific chemo was I now losing her because of a glitch in her medications? Oh, dear God. No!*

I donned my gown outside the BMT unit and pushed through the doors. Nurses were still nearby when I entered Racinda's room. She smiled and said that she was sorry for getting me out of bed. I could tell, though, she was glad to see me.

In fact, everything was fine, and in a few minutes I said good night and left. I returned to bed and a tossing sleep, the taste of fear on my tongue, my mind jumpy, unable to suppress the sound of footsteps descending a stairway.

On Thursday the time for Racinda's stem cell transplant came, and we waited expectantly with her for the precious bag of blood to arrive from the freezer. Roberta's visit was to end early that afternoon, and she didn't want to miss watching the magic life potion pour into her sister's needy body. After lunch a nurse fetched what seemed to be a very small bag of stem cells. To avoid a mistake, a second nurse double-checked to be sure these cells were in fact Racinda's own.

As the rust-colored fluid dripped through the catheter into her bloodstream, we were gleeful with anticipation, as though watching the home team pound the football toward the opponent's goal—we knew we would score; it was just a matter of time. Roberta and I thought we might see a change in Racinda's appearance; a red blush would spread through her cheeks and she would fling off the covers and ask for her walker. But the miracle in the blood would take longer than that.

Another description for this stage of treatment is stem cell rescue. Literally, these young aggressive cells invade the body's comatose cell factory and kick some bone marrow butt. Since the blood counts are very low, it takes a while for the stem cells to produce enough new red and white cells and platelets to raise the body's defense system to an acceptable level.

Roberta would need to wait to hear results via telephone in a week or so. She bent over the bed to say her good-byes, and both women broke into tears. After a final round of Roberta's resounding prayers, I drove her to the airport. Racinda napped, her stem cells initiating the heroic task of reviving her body to meaningful life.

Noelle flew in for a three-day weekend. When she and Allan arrived at the hospital, I intercepted them in the lobby and prepared them for how their mom looked. I told them that considering the severity of the treatment, she was doing well. Unfortunately, she just looked like she was about to die.

The next days were the most difficult of all. The "drama" of the high-dose chemotherapy was over, as was the eagerly anticipated transplant of stem cells. Now we had to spend an unknown number of days waiting, helplessly watching the decimated woman we loved.

On Sunday morning we gathered in the hospital room,

and in lieu of customary worship, watched a video tribute to Rich Mullins, a vagabond Christian singer who had died a year before in a car wreck. Racinda tried bravely to rivet her mind on the screen, but the annoying aftereffects of treatment wouldn't allow it. One of her eyes watered constantly, and a constant stream of drool dribbled from her mouth.

We turned off the video, and the kids and I picked up the usual family banter, perhaps hoping secretly that our humor and health would strengthen Racinda by osmosis. But all wife and mom could do was watch us, her eyes dim, lethargic, scarily vacant. Occasionally she lisped a word or a short sentence.

I wasn't searching for such thoughts but couldn't help wondering, *Have we made some horrible mistake? Just days ago this old, shriveled woman was my laughing, vigorous companion. My God, what have we done?*

Sunk in my own fear, I was not able to take my children aside and gather them in my arms, perhaps allowing them to release the torrent of feelings dammed up inside. I don't know if it's a man thing, or a Swedish gene thing, or just my own unique twisted thing; but especially with sadness, I find it nearly impossible to flow with the emotion of the moment. And when not sure how to respond, I turn to my default setting—cheery stoicism. I could not lead a conversation that might have flushed out some fears. I pretty much failed them as a father except, perhaps, in doggedly standing by their mother.

Allan, young man in training, seemed to take cues from me. Ever the positive one, he grew restless in that hospital room. I understood. I could only guess how I would have borne such trauma at age sixteen.

On Monday morning Noelle prepared to return to college. As she finished packing her bags, some word in our patter finally pierced my stiff facade. I blurted out frustrations, including a petty annoyance with Racinda, then broke apart. "I just can't do it all!" I said, my frustration ending in sobs.

Poor Noelle was speechless; this was a daddy she hadn't seen before. Later she told me she'd understood for the first time that her father was made of the same raw human material as everyone else. And she was frightened; the world was more threatening. Another rock had shifted under her feet.

We regrouped awkwardly. Noelle scrambled for words of comfort. Like a tomcat, after my brief emotional free fall, I landed on my feet. In minutes I was reassembled. But my secret was exposed. Painful as the short term might be, my daughter and I could let our relationship grow—fellow travelers trying to follow the map in the perplexing state of adulthood.

Noelle spent the last morning with Racinda, rubbing lotion into her mom's feet, helping her labor through the physical therapy, reading aloud the stack of comforting Scripture verses, and watching her sleep.

After tearful good-byes, I took Noelle to the airport, and

losing some tears of my own, watched her disappear into the boarding tunnel.

The quickest any patient with Racinda's treatment regimen had engrafted at the BMT was five days. Could she beat that?

We were back playing the patience game. Each day blood was drawn, and we waited eagerly for the blood numbers from the lab. At this point they were extremely low and not moving up.

When she felt a surge of energy, Racinda would sit in the recliner beside her bed. A few times we played a favorite dice game. She fingered the die stiffly, and I fumbled, too, not having played with rubber gloves before. When a die fell to the floor, I would retrieve and douse it with disinfectant before returning it to the table.

On Wednesday the blood test score was a winner. Numbers were up; Racinda was engrafting. This was the sixth day—a near record. We clapped. We prayed. We hugged. With the good news that her body was rejuvenating, Racinda brightened. Hope is the miracle medicine.

Racinda had only one mouth sore, so with characteristic grit, she forced down food to regain strength. The exercise had helped, too, including our BMT two-step that each day had fewer sways and dips. On her own Racinda would shuffle with the walker to the door, stretch onto tiptoes, and peek through the small window into the hallway. She definitely had cabin fever. Finally her rising blood counts permitted a short trip out into the hallway, the first time Racinda had left her room in fifteen days.

Then another setback. A blood clot developed, caused indirectly by the Hickman catheter. After some tests the doctor wasn't too worried, but this meant more medication. And could this add more days to the hospital stay?

Although Racinda's blood counts were creeping up, she remained wobbly and weak. It didn't look like she would leave the hospital anytime soon. I remembered how the doctors had predicted we would be away from home for a month or more. The ordeal was not even half over. Although I kept on my happy face, inside my mood was sinking. *Would we ever get out of this place?*

On Thursday a friend of Racinda's arrived to keep her company for the day. After the doctor's morning round, I planned to leave and work for several hours.

The doctor and his entourage entered and after examining Racinda, he stepped back and said, "We need to be thinking about sending you home."

"What?" I asked, not sure I'd heard him correctly.

"I think if progress continues, she could go home sometime tomorrow. Of course, we have to figure out how she will get the injections for the blood clot. How far do you live from here?"

"An hour's drive, in normal traffic," I told him. The doctor rubbed his chin, evaluating the wisdom of sending Racinda this far away.

And then a serendipity fell from God's hand, as graceful as a leaf parachuting to the earth in autumn. Our friend piped up, "I'm a nurse. I live near Racinda and could give her those shots. In fact, I used to be an oncology nurse."

The doctor smiled. "Well, if you will promise to call if anything happens," he said to me, "you can go home tomorrow if everything goes as planned."

The doctors left and we celebrated. We knew we would have to return daily for blood tests for a week or longer, but instead of having to camp near the hospital, we could go *home*.

I left the hospital, walking out the front entrance into a breathtaking fall morning—blue sky, just a nip of autumn chilling the warm air. I raised an arm high, pumping my fist with glee, then skipped a few steps, saying aloud, "Praise God, praise God. We're going home. We're going home!"

14

❧

Naked and Unashamed

September 1998

ONCE RACINDA LEARNED she might leave the hospital, her
resolve kicked into turbo. Unfortunately, her body was not yet
aligned with her will. On Friday her blood counts hovered
near the danger stage. The doctor was still willing to let her
leave, but only if the blood numbers rallied.

Late in the day the blood still was not cooperating, and
Racinda asked me what we should do. Maybe it was foolish to
try so hard to go home and then return for evaluation the next
morning? I looked into her eyes, much brighter now than
they'd been. They sent the message that mattered: She wanted
out of this place badly.

"No, let's go for it!" I told her. "Even if we're home just
long enough to sleep, at least you will have left the hospital—
you'll be in your own home."

"Thanks, honthey," she said in her lisping voice, giving me
a crooked smile because of lips still numbed by the chemo.

The nurses briefed us on Racinda's continuing vulnerability. Until her blood counts rebounded higher, she must eat carefully—no fresh fruit, for example. Dishes must be washed carefully. No going to public places. All of the precautions were to protect her from bacteria and the infection threats.

As a last-gasp attempt to bump up the blood counts, our nurse brought in a jug of fluid that often gave a BMT patient enough boost in platelet count to escape hospital confinement. The bottle slowly ran dry, and another blood sample went to the lab.

We waited, Racinda's belongings bagged and piled. At around 8:00 P.M. the nurse arrived and told us the blood level was acceptable. We could go.

I helped Racinda dress and carried her items to the car. We hurried, afraid some other medical guru might show up, look at the chart, and say, "Wait a minute! She can't go!"

An attendant and wheelchair arrived. I ran ahead and pulled the van to the hospital entrance. The aide and I helped a stooped Racinda climb aboard and buckle her seat belt. We waved good-bye.

The sun had disappeared over the mountains and night was coming fast. We said little driving south. Wide-eyed Racinda took in the city sights like a released prisoner unfamiliar with life outside the cell.

Too exhausted to speak, we still sensed a new season together had begun. Racinda had survived the BMT. Life was different—still scary, but good.

Naked and Unashamed

Allan was waiting when we arrived. Nala wanted to say hello, too, but since we didn't want Racinda knocked flat by a furry battering ram, the dog watched the homecoming through the window from a deck.

With my help Racinda gingerly mounted the two steps from garage to main floor and shuffled to the family room couch. The house had been prepped by a friend—sinks and countertops cleansed of bacteria with disinfectant, throw rugs lifted so they wouldn't snag Racinda's feet.

Since climbing stairs was about as easy for Racinda as scaling the final stretch up Mount Everest, she would live on the main floor until she regained confidence in her legs.

Allan and I made her bed and Racinda eased in for the night. I placed her walker nearby and left an old schoolmarm's bell on an end table. This would be her means of summoning me during the night from a nearby room.

Soon we were tucked in and I drifted into less than restful slumber. Twice during the night the bell tinkled, my heart shifting into overdrive by the sudden jerk from sleep. I leaped up each time and hustled to her bedside, wondering in what condition I'd find her. We had left the equivalent of an intensive care ward only hours before, so I was nervous. I feared that if I didn't arrive quickly enough, she would somehow haul herself out of bed. But, in such a weakened state, she might fall, and I'd have no choice—because of the threat of internal bleeding—but to take her back to the BMT unit. They would readmit her to the hospital for who knew how long; I couldn't bear the thought.

So I answered her bell like a crazed fireman, but all she needed was an escort to the bathroom. After bedding her down, I would retreat to my bunk and try to will my adrenaline count to a level that would allow sleep.

After morning light filled my room, another sound woke me with a jump. In the hallway, scraping along the wood floor, I heard the unmistakable sliding, wheel-squeaking sounds of Racinda's walker. *Oh no,* I thought. *What is she doing out of bed? Did I not hear the bell?* I lay still, not sure how to respond.

She came closer; I heard the rasping breath. The walker clunked down the one step into my room. With a groan she maneuvered near my bed.

"Honthey?" she said. "Can I have a snubble?"

I laughed. How could I help but love a woman like that, willing to risk serious injury in the quest for a long-missed morning embrace.

I helped her flop and scoot into bed. And we held one another close. Oh my, it sure was good to be home.

The routine in the following days was frustrating and boring. Every morning we drove to the hospital, where Racinda waited in the car while I located a wheelchair. After she strapped on a protective mask, I rolled her to the BMT unit, where a nurse checked her over and drew the daily blood sample. How Racinda felt meant little; the blood counts dictated everything.

The first morning back, her counts had slumped to perilous levels. Another huge bottle of magic medical potion was brought in, and by late afternoon her blood count rebounded and we could go home.

The improvement was steady each day, but Racinda was dependent on the BMT staff. On Thursday the doctor and nurse announced that if we promised to be careful and no problems developed, we could skip hospital visits over the weekend—a three-day one at that. We felt like soldiers granted a surprise leave.

On Friday night we ventured out on a little "date," a stop at a local coffee bar followed by a drive to enjoy the fall evening. Racinda waited in the car while I bought our drinks. In the B.C. days Racinda and I had sometimes stopped here and listened to a woman strumming her guitar and singing melodies from the sixties and seventies.

As I entered on this night, her song jarred loose an emotional landslide. "The night they drove old Dixie down," the lady balladeer wailed. Memories and moods of sweet nights long forgotten swept through me. The melody fell like dew upon my dry soul, reminding me—if only faintly—of times free of blood counts and survival rates. The song itself meant little, but the tune and words were an artery to nights past when life was moist, warm, and fragrant, hanging like a wisp of cloud on a red-smeared sunset.

Not so this season. These were the dry, lean days of a summer sapped by drought, dust scraping the eyes, driven by relentless wind. But the music brought the scent, borne on tender breeze, of coming rain.

I rejoined Racinda in the car. Enticed by a colorful dusk, we drove west toward the mountains, sipping our drinks in quiet, the wheels humming in harmony with the pavement. Existence fell still for me. Pushed aside were a thousand thoughts of pain, shame, worry, regret—all consumed by one ache of longing. Not a desire for moments gone, although this night's sounds had found forgotten alcoves. Nor did I long much for things to come—our future's horizon had not the strength to lift even a mirage. No, this was the rarest of tastes, the fine wine called *this moment.*

An unexpected joy overwhelmed. This was not what was supposed to be. Beside me rode a waif for a wife, her body worn and boiled dry. In her presence, though, I was strangely moved. We were real lovers now, stripped, left naked by circumstances. Disease had shed her of distracted busyness. I had seen rags of selfish obsession ripped away.

We rode quietly, watching the Artist brushing His evening canvas, two people dressed, yet naked except for their essence. A great peace consumed me, not a peace to end all trouble, but a peace that whispered, *You know something about love now . . . and this is good.*

Naked and Unashamed

❧

I suppose Racinda had never needed me more than now. Although every day she pushed toward full recovery, the journey had just begun.

After several frustrating nights with that annoying school bell and not much rest for either of us, we moved to our second-floor room. Now if help was needed she could reach over and tap me—no more bell jolting me from sleep to instantaneous cold sweat. This meant Racinda must make the tortuous climb up one flight of stairs. I steadied her as she slowly lifted one foot at a time. Her hips, in particular, had lost their power.

At first we made only one round trip to the second floor each day. This meant many stair jaunts for me, as I went up and down fetching medicine, ice water, the walker or cane, eyeglasses—you name it—it was always on the other floor!

Not only was Racinda too weak to walk on her own, but she also needed assistance with dressing and bathing. I also helped cleanse and rebandage the Hickman catheter. Most mornings I gave her a sponge bath while she sat in a chair. At this point I felt as though I were caring for her at some future time when we were senior geezers, a situation that provoked much teasing and laughter. Her body may have been temporarily in the shop, but I detected no breakdown in spirit or wit.

Racinda did find strength to comb her hair, a few wisps waving on a denuded plane. In time she gave up on the crop and Allan shaved her head.

After the bath we would work together on getting her dressed. For weeks she didn't have the strength or flexibility to pull on socks and shoes. On my knees I carefully slid on and tied her footwear.

Caring for her was not a burden. At first I felt awkward, helping someone who had always been so competent and self-sufficient. But she offered no resistance, which would have been foolish, because she couldn't do these simple tasks herself. And her sweet resignation to her fate was endearing; I loved helping someone who was so genuinely appreciative. At a level never experienced before in our marriage, I became my wife's servant. And the more I served, the more joy and pride I felt.

During the daytime hours I slipped to my basement office to work. Racinda rested in the room above me, and when she needed help, thumped on the floor with a metal baseball bat.

When Racinda's blood counts reached a safer level, we looked for escapades away from home to flee the boredom.

One soggy afternoon we went to the local high school football stadium to catch a sporting event. I brought my video camera to record the action, and since the two of us huddled atop the bleachers were the only spectators, without embarrassment I could do silly play-by-play gab. Racinda added commentary. We giggled shamelessly at our bad jokes.

Our eyes riveted to a tall lad on the field. We admired his

loping stride, hustle, and skill in passing and receiving. That boy, of course, was Allan, his face flushed red from exertion, alive with pleasure during an afternoon of ultimate Frisbee.

His team, the Pep Band Kids, was wiping up their rivals— the high school club Frisbee team. No cheerleaders, referees, PA announcements, scowling coaches, hot dogs, security guards, or scoreboard. No vein-bloated parents demanding blood—just one mom and dad complaining about rear ends made frosty by frigid aluminum seats, savoring the pleasure as boys (and a few girls, too) ran, and leaped, and laughed, and shouted in triumph as the spinning disk found sure hands in the end zone.

For longer than I want to admit, I wanted Allan's dream to be my dream's child: I would sit in stadium or arena and watch my prodigy score on a keeper or drain the three from beyond the arc . . . and feast on cheers. And if my dream had not retired as Allan's birthed, would I ever have heard notes flowing sweet and sassy from his golden horn? Would I ever have watched my boy at sport like this, romping with friends on the wet green grass, intoxicated by fall air scented with sweat?

Racinda and I shivered until we were blue and left arm in arm, before the last seconds expired on a game too good for a clock.

*

Slowly, sometimes nearly imperceptibly, Racinda recovered. She abandoned the walker, so we gave it back to the BMT unit.

Next the cane was put away. I no longer needed to dress her, except for the socks and shoes, and she showered on her own, sitting on a plastic chair. On one visit to the BMT, Racinda asked that I not get the wheelchair, and she walked proudly, if slowly, all the way from the parking garage.

We went to see the Sheriff, and he explained the final step in her treatment—twenty-five doses of radiation. During our last afternoon at the BMT unit, a nurse pulled the useful, but annoying, Hickman catheter from Racinda's chest.

Her speech slowly returned to normal, but feet and hands stayed numb and unfeeling. Her handwriting scarcely could produce a readable grocery list. For therapy she played the piano, and though the fingers found the right keys, the feel had deserted her music. During one song she thought the foot pedal wasn't working. When she looked, she saw that her foot had slipped from the pedal without her knowing it.

Because of her depleted immune system, we stayed home most of the time. Never had we spent so much time together, but rather than grow tired of the constant companionship, we became increasingly happy, often giggling like preschoolers.

One day Racinda told me that she had fallen in love with me all over again. How crazy was this? We had spent years when times were "good" drifting apart, finding ways to lose our love. Then cancer knocks twice and we become lovebirds? The reasons are sublime and simple—I'll stick with the simple: The cancer woke us up. None of us can live the suburban American deception forever before reality rings the doorbell.

We are finite and frail. Days are numbered. We fade like grass. For somebody, somewhere, this is the last sunrise. So how are we going to live today—while there's time—with the ones we love?

We often sat on a couch side by side, and with TV boring and nothing much to say, I would massage her scalp, searching for signs of reforestation.

"You like to rub my head, don't you!" Racinda said, in surprise and delight.

But even when I nodded my enthusiasm, she would sigh in disappointment, "But I'm just a bald lady!"

No, not just any bald lady. *My* bald lady.

15

❧

Steal Away

October 1998

AFTER BEING HOME FOR WEEKS and near death from cabin fever, on a Saturday we saw a newspaper blurb advertising a concert by a boys' choir at a nearby college. We ditched caution and left for a night on the town—in a crowd.

On that chilly fall evening, we walked slowly across the expansive lawns to the chapel where the choir would perform. I was stunned to enter in Colorado Springs a mini-cathedral, a house of worship built on America's frontier ground, with the majesty of the churches of Europe. The sanctuary was narrow and long, a room of stone, arches, stained glass, and wooden pews. The high ceiling gave room for sounds and spirits to soar.

We made our way down the long aisle at Racinda's speed and found seats. Wearing her hated wig and a wide-brimmed hat, she preferred to sit less noticed near the back.

The church's interior was half-dark, small lights creating an amber-tinged glow.

The choir entered and mounted risers set on the altar. The director raised his arms and the high voices rang out, delicate harmonies floating ecstatically to the roof, like young birds flitting free from the nest.

Racinda and I exchanged looks brimming with wonder. Wasn't this a moment that compelled all struggling earth pilgrims to take another step, to reach forward in spite of pain and terror? Yes, such an exquisite taste as this music, served with love from on high, overwhelmed a bitterness like high-dose chemotherapy.

The boys sang many songs, but a spiritual that first rose from the lips of fleeing slaves loosed shackles in my heart.

"Steal away . . . steal away . . . steal away to Jesus." The agonized melody, the words ripe with longing, for me were a stunning epiphany. Of course! Life here is beautiful, moments of love and music worth all the struggle until the last gasp.

"Steal away . . . steal away . . . steal away to Jesus."

But when this scene ends, because of a love dying for our life, the curtain lifts again.

Steal away . . . steal away . . . steal away to Jesus.

Epilogue
Touching the Shadows

May 2000

ANOTHER WEEKEND FAMILY GETAWAY trip to the mountains.

On Sunday we needed to be home by mid-afternoon, but with several hours to kill, we checked out of our motel in Salida, Colorado, and on a sun-immersed morning went looking for a short hike in the mountains, to savor the hours when spring passes the season to summer.

Racinda and I hold these family moments near now because they are infrequent. In another day Noelle returns to Chicago for a summer psychology internship. Allan, who graduated from high school a week ago, is working full-time at his necessary career of parting from Dad and Mom, the mission complete in August when he leaves for Miami to study music.

With no specific trail in mind, we turned off the highway

near Buena Vista and headed west on a two-lane blacktop toward several of Colorado's "fourteeners," peaks majestic, all looking smug and proud, peering down on our valley from more than fourteen thousand feet.

We stopped at a roadside store for drinks and souvenirs, stopped again at a lake where the fisher people flipped their bobbers and bait into the liquid glass, and then stopped last at a trailhead announcing a path to Agnes Vaille Falls.

Noelle and Allan started ahead of us, still together in post-childhood years, good playmates, now friends, forever-bonded blood. Their pace was brisk, but certainly not too fast for me. I followed eagerly for fifty yards, gaining, then realized that I walked alone. I stopped and turned to see Racinda behind, moving slowly, unable to keep up.

So I waited, sadly more out of duty than desire, my emotions torn again as a thousand times before since the plague arrived three years ago—one part of me wanting to turn and climb fast to catch the children, to enjoy my health and strength. To forget. To deny. And the other part, the one knowing that I am forever promised to someone who on this day—through no fault of her own—just could not walk fast. Again I had to choose how I would live my life.

When Racinda caught up, I walked with her, oh so slowly, watching those two familiar backs disappear up the trail.

And I struggled with resentments—you know them, too, don't you? The "Woe Is Me" tune: *Why, on this perfect morning, as we meet one hiking group after another, all of them walking briskly—dads, moms, kids all smiles and happy health— must I be the one to trudge with feet wanting to fly, restrained by my wife's body? Why is Racinda not stronger? Why this? Why me?*

Yes, the cancer had returned. In fall 1998, after the horrific high-dose chemotherapy and twenty-nine radiation treatments, the straight-shootin' Sheriff had advised us that if the cancer ever came back, most likely it would happen within twelve months and "it won't be pretty." The tumor marker tests went bad in fall 1999, and the rotten stuff was found in Racinda's liver, and our worst nightmares became real daytime events.

One October afternoon, in one of those shrinking examining rooms, the Sheriff closed the door and showed us the CT scan film, and told us that the treatment he could offer no longer ended with the words "Possible cure." Racinda might have weeks or months or . . . maybe longer. And Racinda interrupted, her voice shaking, "Can you please keep me alive until my son's graduation?"

And the Sheriff said gently, his good-guy heart pouring compassion from behind his doctor's badge, "That's what we do—give people as many birthdays, and holidays, and anniversaries as possible."

Racinda did have more chemotherapy, the cancer poison dripping through a tube into her arm. But then her body rose up in allergic reaction, a revolution that left her battered and weakened.

And there's so much more to tell, the story too horrible, too wonderful, too recent. I have not the words.

I will say that when the darkness was about to suffocate, a light broke through. With hope on earth dying, hope in heaven birthed. We reached out with desperate, open hands and asked for a healing touch. And with eyes tender and a smile we'll not forget, the answer came: "Well, of course!"

So on a sparkling morning in May, the birds in fine feather and butterflies fresh from their womb, Racinda still recovering but in health, I had no reason to sing self-pity. But I am so annoyingly human; I wanted *no* burdens.

We walked on, with tiny labored steps. "I don't think I can make it," Racinda said in gasps. "Let's rest."

"No. Lean against me." We turned to look, I below her on the trail, her hands resting on my shoulders. She braced on me, catching her breath, allowing strength to flow into her legs. We consumed God's beautiful work with our eyes. A few high white clouds, the Decorator's touch to make sky a bluer blue. Across the valley, greening aspens and spring-freshened pines merged, a soft quilt to cover all but a mount's craggy face. Snow the cap, its tassel a ribbon browning in warmer canyons.

Revived, we turned, and arm in arm climbed again. With the sun at our back, I noticed our two shadows on the rocky ground, lurching forward in awkward cadence. I thought, *As long as I stay near her shadow, as long as our shadows touch, we will make it.*

A little farther along, she said, "My legs are like marshmallows. Why don't I sit down here and you go on?"

"No, it can't be that far. Can't you hear the falls?"

Epilogue: Touching the Shadows

We both heard the concert of water and rock, so we crept on.

Around the last boulder-filled bend, we saw Agnes Vaille Falls, water high, spurting and crashing, chilled and murky with snowmelt. We selected a rock, and Racinda sat to rest and gaze with clear view. I stood near, our shadows one, still.

Credits

THERE ARE MANY PEOPLE who are important in the journey described in this book. Here I will name some, but many more could join this list—thanks to each of you who have prayed and extended a hand along the way.

My deep appreciation to:

My parents, Florence and Edwin Nygren, faithful in marriage and faith. We shared many winter evenings listening to the wail of wind and rustle of book pages. I love and miss you both.

My brothers and their wives, Dick and Lyn, Irv and Liz, Burt and Julie—for showing a young man what marriage and family look like.

Rachel Aves, for welcoming me as a son into her family.

Dick and Roberta Edgar, for running ahead in faith while we were learning to walk.

Churches along the way, full of supportive pastors and caring brothers and sisters: Bethlehem Evangelical Free Church, Cooperstown, North Dakota; First Federated Church, Des Moines, Iowa; First Presbyterian and Christ Presbyterian,

Nashville, Tennessee; TriLakes Chapel, Monument, Colorado; New Life Church, Colorado Springs, Colorado.

Lawrence Stone, for my start in book publishing. And for others who have aided me in a rewarding career: Sam and Charles Moore, Robert Wolgemuth, Mike Hyatt, John Eames, Ken Stephens, and Rolf Zettersten.

Victor Oliver, my special mentor and friend.

Sandy Fribley, for honest editorial insights and friendship.

Gene Holden—thanks, Pierre, for years of friendship and mogul mastery.

Stephen Sorenson and Doug Van Schooneveld, for companionship while walking to the edge.

Dennis Rainey, for the opportunity to write full-time and feed a family, too—what a guy and boss.

Ben Bartholemew, for golf therapy.

Dr. Cal and Mimi Wilson, for splendid lodging during the BMT ordeal.

The many friends who helped so much during the cancer saga—but special thanks to Ann and Dick Crowell, Louise Deaton, Nan and Charles Doolittle, Tom and JoAnn Doyle, Chris McCloy, Lydia Peek, Dave and Rosalyn Sample, Bill and Ruth Stone, and Stephanie Stone.

Feeders of Allan during BMT days: Ben and Debbie Bartholemew, Al and Mimi Brown, Paul and Barb Matzat, and Carolyn and Phil Saletta.

Insights into the interior life: Nita Baugh Andrews, Brent Curtis (posthumously), Dan Allender, and Susan Hykes.

Credits

For the loving care and concern of dozens of physicians, nurses, and other health professionals throughout the United States—with special thanks for the compassion and friendship of Dr. Ray and Liz Strand.

Shelley Webb, Ron and Donna Poelstra, Dave and Joyce Dickinson—partners in prayer and power.

Rob Van Cura—Best Village Inn breakfast buddy.

Faithful channels of the grace, mercy, and healing of Christ: Kim and Joe Galindo and Robert Mawire.

Steele County Press, Finley, North Dakota, for the first *real* ink.

Franklin Graham—what can I say!

Kathy Helmers, agent, for believing that even old editors can write.

My editors at Thomas Nelson: Janet Thoma (for launching a former comrade) and Anne Trudel (careful and reliable in all things).

Jesus, no better friend.

My daughter, Noelle—early encourager on this work, truck driving partner, awesome hugger, and beautiful woman of God.

My son, Allan—computer medic, best five iron in the West, steady in trials, and heavenly music maker.

Racinda—you kept your end of the bargain; now I've kept mine. Love always.

About the Author

BRUCE NYGREN is a native of North Dakota. He holds a B.A. in Social Science from the University of North Dakota. After completing his service in the U.S. Army, including a stint in South Vietnam, he earned an M.S. in Mass Communications from Iowa State University.

Bruce has spent his entire professional career in publishing-related activities. He first worked for the Des Moines *Register* and *Tribune* newspapers. After this he entered the book publishing industry, where he has worked since 1977.

While employed by Thomas Nelson Publishers, Bruce held numerous positions, including acquisitions editor and vice president of book editorial. Bruce also worked for NavPress, Colorado Springs, as the editorial director.

Currently he is employed as senior editor and writer for FamilyLife Ministry, based in Little Rock, Arkansas. He is the coauthor of two books, *Child of Rage* and *101 Ways to Your Husband's Heart,* and has assisted others with numerous books.

Bruce and his family live in Colorado. He may be contacted by e-mail at BANygren@aol.com.